MOM'S SECRET LOVER

SECOND CHANCE FOR FIRST LOVE

BETH LOURE

CHAPTER 1

ecca

WHEN THE KNOCK FINALLY ARRIVES, I'm still standing by the full-size mirror in the master bedroom admiring my slim figure, newly acquired thanks to the sexy corset I'm wearing. That's *all* I'm wearing. Well, that and a sheer pair of panties and knee-high boots.

Knock-knock-knock.

"Just a minute!" I yell and rush to the front door as quickly as the 4-inch stilettos of the boots allow.

My ample bosom bounces with every step as the heels answer the *knock-knock-knock* with *tap-tap-tap.* I love that sound. It's the music of foreplay.

The hinges screech as I open the door, and there she is. The love of my life, smiling wide. Showing the world that big sexy gap between her upper teeth. Four months together, and I still shiver every time our eyes meet.

Lia's doe-like eyes widen when she sees me wearing the

corset set and boots she gave me on our three-month anniversary. She glances down at my body and exhales loudly, almost whistling her appreciation. That's exactly the response I was craving.

"Hey, baby," she says softly. "You look gorgeous."

"You too," I say, although I think that she looks tired. It's understandable—she just taught five aerobic classes back to back, after all. It doesn't matter; I still find her breathtaking.

She's wearing a sports outfit under her opened coat—a cropped fuchsia top, pink Capri leggings, and tennis shoes. She came straight from class, which is exactly what I asked her to do when I invited her over. I'm so happy she obliged, and I'm grinning so hard my jaw hurts.

I lean over and inhale her scent as I pull her inside. I love the way she smells after a long day at the gym. It's a combination of sweat and latex and something else. I think it's the smell of her energy, her vitality. It's the smell of her life force, and it makes me crave her like crazy. She's standing on her toes, reaching up toward me with her lips slightly parted. She's four foot eleven, and I'm towering over her with my five foot seven. I'm her sweet giantess.

I move my lips close to hers with the intention to kiss her softly, a welcome greeting. But the second our lips meet, it's like a chemical reaction. They're locked together. All our longing goes into that kiss. It's deep and passionate, and it intensifies when Lia puts her arms around my neck and pulls me down. She wraps a toned leg around my waist. I bend my knees, and she wraps the other one around me as well. Now I'm carrying her.

Her mouth is warm and soft. So soft, it's like kissing a cloud. I melt a little on the inside.

I slide my hands under her coat and grab her firm buttocks. My breasts press against hers, and I push my tongue deep into her mouth. She makes an ecstatic low sigh.

That little sound makes my knees wobble. Afraid that I'm going to drop her, I kneel down on the rug, and now we're on our knees, kissing and fondling each other. I want to touch her everywhere.

We're still by the door. At least we managed to close it behind us.

I'm sliding down until I'm lying on my back. Lia straddles me. I stare at her beautiful face as she concentrates on pulling the strings that hold my corset in place.

She's so gorgeous with her hair—a mess of a bun with loose hanks that curl by her ears—stiff with sweat after hours of working out and her dark brown eyes and the little concentration crease in the middle of her forehead.

I pull the pin that holds her hair in place. It falls over her face, long, silky, and lush. I comb my fingers through it.

"Hey!" Her eyes meet mine. "What are you doing?"

I smile. She's so cute when she's a little cross. Her eyes are all fiery, and her lips are curled up in a sweet, child-like pout.

"I missed your stupid duck-face," I say. My voice is hoarse.

She leans down and kisses me on the cheek. Her lips touch my skin ever so lightly, but they burn my flesh. I close my eyes and give in to the sweet sensation. She slides her lips along the column of my neck, barely touching the skin. I can feel her warm breath as she exhales. I'm burning with desire.

Her fingers are fidgeting with the lace strings of the corset again. Her breath is getting shorter, and I can feel her frustration building up as the damn things don't budge. "It's all tangled up!" she cries.

She's so sweet. I frame her face with my palms and caress her cheekbones with my thumbs. "You're so pretty," I coo. I still find myself in awe sometimes, unable to believe that this goddess is attracted to plain old me.

"I want to say 'hi' to my girls!" she pouts, her hands

squishing my breasts. I can barely feel a thing above the thick fabric.

"Let me do it, baby." I try to unravel the knots, but she doesn't let go.

"It's a stupid, stupid thing, and I hate it!"

My laugh offends her. I can see it in her pressed lips.

Lia is impulsive and moody, like a pussycat. She can be sweet one minute, and in the next, bite your head off, exactly as a cat would.

Now, she's leaving me aroused and breathless on the rug. The make-out session has ended abruptly. I sigh deeply. It's as if my whole body is protesting. I want her to come back to me, but she's already on the move.

I watch her as she goes down the hall. I just love her gait. It's like she's walking on lava or hot coals, all springy and light. Her hair jumps with every step. I could look at her forever without getting bored.

I still watch her while I'm trying to get up. It's not easy to maneuver with those heels. I hope she's not looking at me when I wiggle myself ungracefully to an upright position.

She isn't. She's already in the kitchen.

Remembering the state of my kitchen, I hurry after her, slightly ashamed.

"Oh," she says with pure delight when she notices the mess. It's a sink full of dirty dishes and counters full of crumbs. It's the mess of a week's worth of breakfasts and quick dinners that Rachel and I grabbed between work commitments.

"You cooked! I love it when you cook for me." Lia gets the wrong impression. Her eyes are glistering with pure joy, and I can feel the disaster that's about to happen. She opens the fridge, excited like a little girl anticipating the discovery of a birthday cake.

Damn it.

"Oh." Lia's voice is disappointed when she realizes how empty the fridge is. "So you have *nothing* edible? I don't believe it! When you invited me over for a romantic evening, I assumed that included a meal." Her tone is biting

I chuckle. "Yeah. I guess I should have thought about that. Sorry, baby. I invested all the time I had on the main course." I finally get the corset to open up. I slide it down my torso. "Come and get it."

"I'm hungry, Bex, damn it. I'm absolutely famished!"

I lay on the couch, one leg on the backrest and the other on the floor. The sheer lace thong exposes everything. I feel sexy lying like that, with the corset hugging the flab in my middle section. "Dinner is served," I say with a seductive tone.

Lia looks at me and gasps. My heart misses a beat seeing her reaction to my pose. She rushes over. *Lava, lava, lava.* And she's here, kneeling beside me. Her hot, precious lips land on my wanting mouth while her thumb and index finger rub a nipple. My whole body is tickled, and my hands fly to her hair.

Lia's lips leave mine, and I instantly miss her sweetness, but then she gently bites my nipple. Her hand slides over my mound and underneath the tiny thong. She hovers over my clit with the tip of her index finger. It's so good. I arch my back and raise my buttocks toward her.

"Yeah, baby," I moan. Her fingers tap my slit. Within seconds, I'm ready to go over the top.

But then she stops. I open my eyes and articulate my objection. "Hey!"

She smiles a malicious smile. Oh, the gap between her upper teeth.

"Don't stop," I whisper. "You can't stop now."

She leans over and bites my lower lip. Teasing.

I raise my head and suck her mouth while trying to direct

her hand back into my folds, but she's stronger than me. I can't make her do what she doesn't want to do.

"Come on, Bex. Let's eat first," she whispers into my ear before nibbling an earlobe.

"Yeah," I say with my husky voice. "Let's eat pussy."

She laughs and holds my face between her hands. She looks me in the eye. "I've created a beast," she says before kissing me on the forehead. "Seriously, Bex. I need to get some proteins into my body, like pronto. And since your idea of a romantic evening means nothing but sex, I'm going to order in for the both of us."

I'm so disappointed. I've been fantasizing about this evening for a long time, and now it's ruined.

"Baby, we don't have much time. Rachel is supposed to be back around nine."

"So?"

Her question makes me mad. She's asking just to spite me. I count to ten before I answer.

"So, by the time the food gets here, we could barely squeeze in a quickie!"

She shrugs. "Well, that's what you get for keeping me a secret."

She orders veggie burgers with steamed beans and low carb buns. *Yuck.* Well, that's what you get when you date a nutritionist.

I watch her while she's ordering. She twists a hank of her hair around her index finger while she paces the room. No lava in her gait. When she's finished, she stands there, looking at me. She's like a doe caught in headlights. Only hotter.

"Have you told your friends about us?" she asks. Her voice is sharp.

We had a different version of this conversation last week, and now, when she's hungry and tired, is definitely not the right time to revisit the subject. This is going to end badly. I must diffuse this "coming out" bomb before it explodes. "Speaking of friends, how's what's-his-name that fractured his knee in Kickbox class? Maybe we should pay him a visit, poor guy."

She doesn't take my bait. "What about your co-workers, Bex? Have you told them about us?"

"Baby, you know I want to shout my love for you from the rooftops, but I need to tell Rachel first. You know that."

"And when are you going to tell your daughter?"

"Soon."

"Like today, soon? Or tomorrow? Maybe next week? Next month?" Her pitch climbs higher and higher as she speaks.

I try to stay calm. "She's going through a phase right now, and—"

"She's always going through a phase!"

"Well, yeah, she's a teenager. That's what they do. Remember how you were at nineteen?"

She looks disappointed, and it pains me to see her like that. It hurts to know I'm the reason for her pain. Guilt overwhelms me and I wince a little. But I'm in an impossible position. Whatever I do will hurt someone.

"Baby, I want to tell Rachel. I *will* tell her. I just need to find the right time."

She doesn't say anything, just looks at me. There are tears in her eyes.

"Come on, baby," I say and spread my arms in a desperate attempt to end this stupid feud. "She'll be home soon. And I don't want to waste our precious time together fighting."

Now she's all fiery. "So, you got me here on a fake promise for a romantic evening, while all you were planning was to have a quick fuck then throw me out before your daughter came home."

Ouch. It sounds so selfish when she says it like that.

"I'm not your sex toy, Becca! I have feelings too, you know." She calls me Becca only when she's really mad.

"I know that, Lia! I'm sorry. Come on, baby, give me some credit!"

"You didn't even ask me about my day. Which was crappy, by the way, thank you. You open the door wearing that," she gestures toward my corset and boots. "You don't have food in the house, well, except that junk you shouldn't be eating in the first place."

"That's Rachel's," I say then hurry to add, "Sorry."

She's not done yet.

"What am I supposed to think, Becca, huh? What am I supposed to think?" She's counting my crimes on her fingers. "You keep our relationship a secret, all you want is sex—I'm getting the feeling I'm some kind of a mistress here, Bex, and I truly don't like it."

All I can hear is that she called me Bex, which means I still have room to wiggle inside this argument.

"I'm sorry, Lia. You're right. I was selfish and thoughtless, but that's only because I've missed you so much." Our work schedules have made it impossible to meet for almost two weeks.

She shakes her head and marches toward the door. When she reaches it, she turns back toward me and gives me an intense look. I just need to say the right words, and she'll stay.

"Lia," I say quietly. I put all my love into my voice. "Please. Don't go." I can see the hesitation written all over her pose. She breaks eye contact.

"Dinner is on its way," I say. "Let's just eat and chat. No sex. Just hang out."

She looks back into my eyes. Oh dear god, she's so hot when she's furious. Her small breasts rise up and down as she breathes. Her chiseled abs look like someone sculpted them in stone.

"When are you going to tell her about us?" she asks through gritted teeth. "I need a time frame here, Bex."

"Soon, sweetie, I swear. As soon as I can." I put my hands on my chest.

"When?" she demands.

"When the time is right."

She looks at me, and I can tell that she wants to come back and settle this.

"Look, baby," I say with my softest tone. "You're not a mom, so you don't know how it goes."

Bam. She slams the door behind her.

I hit myself on the forehead. Damn. Why did I say that? I rush to the door. Tap-tap-tap my heels go. It takes forever. I don't care that I'm half-naked and the neighbors might see. "Lia!" I yell.

It's no use. She's already gone.

achel

THE FLORESCENT LIGHT in the poetry section is flickering. It's been like that since I started working here six months ago. Nobody seems to care but me. Mrs. Ilman, the head librarian, says there are more pressing matters than investing funds in a broken light fixture in the most deserted section of the public library.

The unsteady light flashes in the corner of my eye as I sit on a step ladder trying to decipher Sylvia Plath's *Ariel*. I can't figure out what she wanted to say in this poem, but it doesn't take even one inch off its beauty. A long shadow casts over me, appearing and disappearing as the lights wink on and off. I know it's her—Mrs. Ilman. I don't bother to take my nose out of the book when I speak.

"I'm just taking a short break, Mrs. Ilman. Everything is all set for tonight, and I'll be there in a jiffy."

Jiffy is Mrs. Ilman's favorite word. When I say it quietly and politely, she gives me a nod and an approving grunt. I guess that it's going to buy me an extra five minutes with Sivvy.

Then a voice which is clearly not Mrs. Ilman's says, "Interesting choice you got there. 'Melts in the wall. And I am the arrow,'" she recites from the poem I'm reading. Now I have to see who it is.

I raise my eyes from the book and, for a brief second, I'm blind. It's like a ray of sunshine has found its way to the darkest aisle in the library. I'm overwhelmed by the beauty of the woman standing there.

Her crystal-green eyes are so bright, they're almost transparent. Her jawline is square and curves down to a round chin. Her lips, colored in orange, are spread in a smile. Small earrings sparkle on her earlobes. And her hair—well, it's a masterpiece of black, layered pixie with blond forelock and edgy fringes. Only strong and confident women can wear this kind of hairdo without looking ridiculous.

"So, you're Rachel," she's reading my name tag.

I push my sleeves down over my palms.

"You certainly have the hair for a Rachel," she says, still smiling. She gestures toward my face for clarification.

I stare. My hair is wavy and falls over my face. I don't style it at all. She comes closer and grabs a piece of it.

"Rachel Green? *Friends?*" she asks while giving it a little tug.

I keep staring.

"Never mind." Her tone changes and her eyes suddenly seem darker. "Mrs. Ilman sent me—"

Then I get it. "Oh, *Friends*! Sorry, I haven't seen that show." My voice is high-pitched and creaky. I hate the sound of it.

She smiles. "Yeah. Well. What was I thinking, a young one like you? You weren't even born when the show ended."

"I'm nineteen." Creak.

"Of course you are."

I don't know how to respond to that. It doesn't matter anyway because she keeps on talking. "Anywho, I'm Sarah Walters. I'm here for the Spoken Word event." She's holding a flier.

I swallow the "yes" that stands on the tip of my tongue. No need to be heard. I nod and jump off the step ladder.

The Spoken Word event is my baby. It took me three weeks to persuade Mrs. Ilman to let me have it, and three more months of hard work to set it up. The flier she's holding I single-handedly designed, printed, and spread all around town because Mrs. Ilman said there was no budget for fliers.

And here I am, the night of, half an hour before it's about to start, hiding in the poetry section because I'm sure this night is going to be a complete failure.

"Mrs. Ilman said I should talk to you about performing tonight. She also mentioned that you'd be hiding in here."

The pretty woman, Sarah Walters, smiles at me again. Her smile is warm and friendly, and I smile back. *Sarah Walters.* Her name sounds familiar. Did I see her slams on YouTube?

I nod fiercely. I'm so ashamed of my voice right now.

Her eyes are glistening. Her energy is contagious. She reminds me why I wanted to have this event in the first place. Inspiration. There's nothing better than to feel inspired; it's like an orgasm of the mind. You feel an infinite amount of energy charging you with hope and happiness. You're sharp and bright, and there's an electrical storm of ideas shooting inside your head, *boom boom boom*. Inspiration. That's my drug of choice. And you can only get it—well, without using any substances—when you're in the presence of creative people.

The tips of my fingers tingle. Something is happening to me, and it's because of this woman. The wheels shift in my brain, and I'm on the verge of an insight when—

"Rachel!" Mrs. Ilman's deep voice startles me. "Oh, there you are," she says as she appears around the corner from the self-help section. "I have an emergency at home, and I must leave, now. Will you be all right tonight by yourself? Can you handle it?"

I nod. Chase should be here any minute now. He promised to help.

"What's not to handle?" wonders the pretty lady, Sarah Walters.

Mrs. Ilman leans over and whispers something in her ear.

I know she's saying I'm unstable. Crazy. I've heard her say it before. "She's a troubled young girl," she said to another librarian when she thought I couldn't hear her.

I'm so humiliated when she does that, I wish the earth would open up and swallow me whole. I wish I could just yell at her. Tell her to shut the fuck up. But that would probably have the opposite effect. That would only prove that she has a point, that I *am* crazy. With my childish voice, I'd be like a kindergartner throwing a tantrum. So I keep my mouth shut. I pull my sleeves down over my palms and hold them tight in my fists. Tears fill my eyes. I try hard to push them down. I don't want to give Mrs. Ilman the satisfaction of seeing me cry. I hate the way she treats me, but I hate my weakness even more. *Damn it.* Tears. I wipe them with my sleeve-covered palms.

"Alright, then." Mrs. Ilman straightens her brown wool skirt. "Break a leg tonight, as they say," she says and gives me a patronizing look before she walks away. She's full of self-righteousness, and I hope *she'll* fall down the stairs and break a leg. It doesn't happen, of course. She takes the elevator.

"Pfff," Sarah Walters says, smiling. "That woman is so full of it, right?" She mimics Mrs. Ilman's gait. I shrug as if I don't care.

That brief moment of revelation I had before Mrs. Ilman's arrival evaporates forever, replaced with the sudden urge to close myself in a bathroom stall and cut. I pull my sleeves down again, hard.

Sarah Walters looks at me funny, and I can't stand it. I want her to go away. But she just stands there as if she's waiting for something. And then I remember. She wants to read tonight. I clear my throat. *Right.*

The list of tonight's performers is in my pocket. It's wrinkled and ragged from too much folding and unfolding, writing and rewriting. There are five names on my list. I add hers at the bottom. She'll be the last performer. I show it to her.

She smiles. "Perfect. I love to be the closing gig." She's still standing next to me.

Why isn't she leaving? What else does she want from me? I need to call Chase. Find out what's keeping him; he was supposed to be here by now. I need him desperately. But I can't call when she's near me, listening.

I hope she'll get the social cue when I take my phone out. Isn't it enough of a hint that our conversation is over? I text Chase, *Where R U?!*

She's still here; I can feel her presence.

"Rachel," she says. Her voice is soft. "I didn't see your name on the list. Why is that? You're a poet too, right?"

I gasp. How on earth does she know that? I haven't told a living soul about my writing. Not even my therapist. Slightly panicked, I touch my pocket. Did I accidentally pull out the wrong piece of paper?

No. It's still there. Folded and folded again into a tiny scrap that fits into the small change pocket in my jean. I shake my head.

"Right. What was I thinking? You clearly aren't ready yet," she says, as if to herself. She turns and walks away. I go after her, trying to step exactly in the same spots. I don't know why I'm doing it, but it feels like I have to.

There are people sitting in the gathering area. Actual people. Some are teenagers, others could easily be my grandparents. There are more people hanging around the refreshments table, making coffee or nibbling chips.

I can't believe there's such a nice turnout. *It's really happening!* Suddenly, I worry there aren't enough chairs. I scan the crowd, trying to count them.

Mia Alfonse is sitting in the front row. We studied chemistry together in our senior year in high school. I didn't know she was into poetry. I squint and hide when she looks back.

I need to tell Chase about it. Where is he? He hasn't replied to any of my texts, and he's not picking up his phone.

What do I do now? I can't go up there on my own.

The evening is doomed. I'm so disappointed. All the hard work I've put into it. The fliers, the refreshments. Tears fill my eyes again. It's so frustrating. If I go up there and speak, my voice would be the joke of the day. But if I don't, there won't be an event. I'll be deeply humiliated no matter which path I choose. I stand at the edge of the seating area, shifting my weight from foot to foot, trying to come up with a solution to this chaos of a situation. I glance at my phone every two seconds to see if Chase has replied, check the entrance to see if he's coming in. My stomach hurts. I need to pee. I need to barf.

"Having cold feet?" It's Sarah Walters. She's standing behind me, whispering in my ear. I nod slightly

She puts her hands on my shoulders. I'm shaking.

"Would you like me to get the evening going? Present the first poet?"

"Please," I whisper. When I speak softly without vibrating the vocal cords, my voice doesn't sound too bad. "Can you present all of them?" My fingers shake as I reach into my pocket and take out the wrinkled list of performers. Just then, it occurs to me that I should have rewritten it on a clean piece of paper and added some information about each performer.

"Wait a sec," I whisper again. I grab a fresh sheet of paper from the printer and quickly jot down a short introductory paragraph about each performer.

"That looks like a fine set," Sarah says when I hand it to her. "I'll try to do my best." She squeezes my arm.

"Thank you."

She walks over to the stage area, which is just a corner with a spotlight and a microphone on a stand.

"Evening, all," she says. "Thanks for coming tonight to a very special Spoken Word event in our local library. I'm Sarah Walters, and I'll be your host this evening. We have a great set for you tonight, but before we start, I would like to thank the head librarian, Mrs. Ilman, who couldn't be with us tonight due to unforeseen circumstances. Thank you for letting us have this intimate gathering."

Scattered clapping follows her announcement. I shrink a little in my seat. I'm not sure if she's going to mention my name too. I want to get credit, but I don't want to have all those eyes scrutinizing me.

"Tonight, we'll hear six original works, written by six different poets, myself included. I hope you'll all sit back and get inspired by our words."

My heart misses a beat when she says the word *inspired*. It's like she's read my mind.

"... And now, without further ado, let's welcome Leo Gastiny with his poem titled *Pickles*."

I sit in the last row, at the very end. I listen to Leo, who slams about his dog, Pickles. It's a long and boring poem. People hide their yawns.

At some point, when I can't take it anymore, I Google Sarah Walters on my phone. Her picture shines at me. The first result is a Wikipedia page. She must be a big shot to have that. I read the whole page. She's won some prizes and was even selected as one of the 'Top 30 Under 30 in Literature' last year. She's way out of the league for this local, no-pay event. I'm so grateful she decided to come.

The next slammer isn't much better than Leo Gastiny. It's Ada Amour, probably a stage name. She talks about Donald Trump. Some people leave.

I squirm in my seat. This is not how I imagined this

evening. At least they're stopping by the donation box and dropping something in. That's cool.

Now and then, I look at my phone. There's nothing from Chase. Not a word. I don't know if I should be worried or angry. It's not like him to be a no-show.

Out of the six performers, five range from mundane to cliché. And then it's Sarah Walkers' turn to slam. The crowd has thinned significantly, which is a shame because she's glorious.

She talks about being a gay person in a straight society. She's funny and smart as she rhymes about her misfortunate sexual experiences and unrequited loves. She knows how to hold the crowd. I laugh and cry, and laugh and cry again. I cheer when she's done, clapping so hard my palms hurt, and I yell, "Bravo! Bravo!" I don't care that people can actually hear me because she was so inspiring with the way she exposed herself, and I want to be like her.

The ten people that stayed until the end get up. They look excited, including Mia Alfonse, who walks by me and says, "Hi Rach," nonchalantly, as if we're friends. I don't answer because I don't want to start a conversation. I don't want to answer questions like, "What are you doing right now?" and "Why aren't you in college?" And I certainly don't care about Mia Alfonse's life.

There's $150 in the donation box. I take out $50 to spread between the other slammers and hand Sarah the rest.

"Great performance," I say. I sound so corny and banal. Those words don't describe what I feel. I want to give her smart and funny and inspiring feedback. "I should have known you're a lesbian," I hear myself say. She gives me a weird look with one eyebrow raised. "You certainly have the hair for it," I joke lamely.

She passes her hand through her blond crest. "Thanks. I guess," she shrugs.

Damn. "Sorry," I mumble. My voice is even higher and creakier than usual. "I... I thought it would be funny because you mentioned my hair before—"

She waves, signaling *it's fine, don't worry about it.* She hands me a card. "I'd love to read your poetry sometime. Call me." And then she does the most surprising thing. She leans over and hugs me. She smells like lavender and lilies.

ecca

By 9 P.M. the kitchen is sparkling clean, and the sexy outfit is stored safely away in my closet. If only I could clean my mind as easily as I sweep the house. I'm still pretty agitated from the way the night unfolded. My usual remedy for heartache is watching *Grey's Anatomy* on Netflix, but it doesn't help; I can't find a comfortable spot on the couch.

I don't have any nails left. I've bitten them all off, which means it's time for that chocolate chip ice cream that's been sitting in the freezer. I'm a big, fat cliché. But I don't care. I need my comfort food. Hell, I deserve it.

Time isn't passing. I look at my phone every 30 seconds in the vain hope of a reply to all the *sorries* I've been texting Lia. Rachel should be home any minute now. My ears are tuned to the door. The second she steps inside, I'm going to say, "Rachel honey, please sit down, we need to talk." And then I'll tell her I have a girlfriend. I've rehearsed the speech in my head for the past 30 minutes, trying to predict Rachel's reaction and prepare for all sorts of questions. There's a knot in my stomach; it gets tighter by the minute.

Rachel has met Lia only once, when the two of us took a personal training class with her. Rachel didn't like Lia. I can still remember her facial expression when she said that Lia had the appeal of a serial killer. My heart sinks every time I think of it.

What will I do if Rachel won't accept my relationship with Lia? What if I'm forced to choose between them? I would never renounce my daughter, but I could never forgive her for rejecting the love of my life.

The tight knot in my belly doesn't loosen up by my stress-eating. Now I'm bingeing. Carrot sticks, expired Greek yogurt, canned soup, microwaved popcorn. Nothing seems to fill me.

My mind drifts. How lovely it would be if everything goes smoothly and Rachel gives me her blessing. Lia could spend the night. I shiver at the thought of waking up next to her warm body. It makes me feel so hot that I need to lie down and masturbate.

Maybe this will relax me. I imagine it's Lia's fingers exploring my folds, her tongue flicking over my clit. It doesn't take long before my whole body convulses, and the wave of my orgasm shakes my body. But it's not as satisfying as having sex with Lia. I crave her more after I'm done. And I'm still stressed out.

I text her. Again. This time I write, *going to tell Rachel tonight!*

It's already 9:15 p.m., and there's no sign of my daughter. I look out the front window; the street is empty. My call goes straight to her voicemail. I don't leave a message.

I try to recall her exact words when she told me she was going to be late. She'd said, "Mom, I have this thing at the library. I'll be home around nine." I didn't listen to what she said next. Instead, I'd rejoiced, thinking, *I'll have the house to myself, and I can ask Lia to come over*. My guilt is excruciating. What kind of a mother am I, preferring my own sexual pleasures over my only child?

I've known Lia only a few months, yet the connection we have is so much deeper and stronger than the one I had with Jason, and we were married for eighteen years.

Overwhelmed with my love for Lia, I know I must tell Rachel. There's no way around it. And then I'll have to figure out a way to share the news with the rest of the world. Especially my colleagues. I'm not ashamed, but I am worried. CPA firms are conservative by nature. What will my clients say? Will they think of me differently, knowing I'm dating a woman? And what will happen to my promotion? In a few months, I'm supposed to become a partner. It's against the law to discriminate employees based on their sexual preferences, but would they still have me in an executive position? What if they find another excuse to fire me?

My thoughts are taking me to dark places, and there's nothing edible left in the house.

There's also no sign of Rachel.

Rachel will freak out. I remember that horrible day when I came home from work and found her leaning over the sink. Her wrists were dripping blood, but she didn't mind that. She was looking at her reflection with crazy eyes. She insisted that it wasn't a suicide attempt, but she couldn't explain what it was or why she'd done it.

She's better now, medicated. But what if she has another fall because her mom's dating a woman? I can't bear that thought. *I can't tell her about Lia*. Not until I know for sure she won't take it the wrong way.

But then again, I'll lose Lia. And I love her so much. I can see myself growing old with her, side by side, two gray ladies, having sex. The vision makes me chuckle. Ever since Lia entered my life, I've been in a constant state of arousal. I just can't get enough of her.

9:30 p.m. Where the hell is Rachel? She doesn't answer her phone; she doesn't reply to my texts. Lia doesn't reply my texts either, and I begin to think maybe there's something wrong with my phone.

I call Jason. He picks up immediately. So it's not my phone.

Jason sounds tired. He's remarried now and doesn't seem to be better off.

"Hey, Jace, I just wanted to check in with you. Have you talked to Rachel lately?" I try to sound casual.

Once, he knew how to read my nuances. His instincts haven't rusted.

"What's wrong, Becca?" He's sharp. Straight to the point. *Damn.*

"Nothing's wrong, I'm just wondering. She's been so secretive lately."

"Yeah, well, I wouldn't know. She hasn't talked to me since I told her we're expecting."

"Renee is pregnant?"

He hesitates for a minute.

"Yeah. I thought you knew. Four months."

I smile to myself, thinking about the last four months of my life. "Congrats. You're going to be a dad again."

"Yeah, I guess." He doesn't sound enthusiastic. "But, Rachel, you think she's depressed?"

I weigh my words. He doesn't know about the wrists incident. Rachel was over eighteen at the time. The hospital didn't have a legal obligation to report it to her father, and she swore me to secrecy.

"I wouldn't say depressed per se, but something is definitely going on with her. Let me know if she talks to you, okay?"

Renee speaks hysterically in the background. "Who is it, Jason? Who are you talking to?"

"I have to go," he says hurriedly. He sounds defeated, and I pity him.

By 10:30 p.m. I'm barely holding on by a thread. Rachel isn't home yet, and I'm worried sick. There are sweat circles under my pits. I pace between the window and the couch and imagine her lying in a ditch somewhere. My fingers hover over 911, but I can't call and say my nineteen-year-old is an hour and a half late. No one would take me seriously. I would probably sound like crazy Renee. I text Lia instead.

Rachel isn't home yet. So worried!!!!!

She doesn't reply, and I know she hasn't read it. She hasn't read any of my messages.

Then Rachel enters, and she's walking on a cloud. She's so happy, and that drives me crazy. How can she be happy when I'm so concerned I can barely function? And I lose it completely. I yell at her like a madman.

"Where the hell have you been?" I don't wait for an answer because I don't really care. I just want her to know how she's made me feel. "I was worried sick about you!" I shout. "I was going to call the police!"

I know I shouldn't be yelling at her. She's practically a grown-up, and I won't achieve anything by yelling. But this evening has brought me to the edge. So I dig out old, motherly worries and slam her with those too.

"Why don't you go to college? When are you going to figure out your life?"

Rachel yells. She waves her hands at me, her eyebrows squinted, "I don't want to be like you. An unhappy divorcee who's slouching on the couch and eating whatever. What's with you, Mom? Stop yelling at me to figure out my life and start figuring out yours!"

It sits at the tip of my tongue—I'm going to shout out that I've fallen in love. I open my mouth to tell her all about Lia when she rolls up her sleeves and shows me her scars. "That's my future, Mom," she says, and I can't say anything after that.

achel

I'm STILL high on inspiration when I finish arranging the chairs and the library is back in place. I'm bursting with creative energy, and I'm not ready to call it a day. So I write.

I'm documenting tonight's events in my journal when suddenly the quietness of the dark library freaks me out. It's vast and cold and lifeless. I feel so alone.

I rush outside. Energy level still high, I run past the bus stop and plan to stop at the next one, but I just keep jogging from stop to stop, telling myself I'll definitely stop at the next one.

It's a bright night. The chilly air is fresh and crisp, and the streetlights pave the curb with patches of light, like an elegant quilt. My jog slows to a trot. Car headlights make me see the world a bit differently as they pass by. The run-down gray concrete streets which I normally don't care about look mysteriously romantic and I take out my notebook to jot down my thoughts, writing manically between bursts of lights. Anything feels possible. I'm elated, euphoric even. I wish this walk would never end. And I don't stop even when I'm tired and thirsty, and my feet hurt.

I'm still floating in awe when I get home. I want to dance and sing and even hug and kiss my mom. She's sitting on the couch wearing sweats which are full of stains and crumbs. I see empty food packets all around her. Seeing her like that drains my energy in an instant. And when she turns her head to give a quick glance at the wall clock, I realize she's been waiting for me. I feel like a child late for curfew.

"Where have you been? It's half past ten!" she yells.

I shrug. "Nowhere. The library."

She knows nothing about the Spoken Word event. I didn't tell her because I didn't want her input. She tends to be very judgmental when I choose to do things she doesn't like or understand, and poetry definitely falls into both the "don't understand" and "don't like" categories.

"Why are you lying to me? The library has been closed for hours! I know that for a fact." She gets up from the couch and starts pacing the room. Her arms are crossed over her chest.

"Yeah. I'm the one who closed it. Told you. We had a thing."

"So where have you been until now? I've been worried sick about you. I've called you like a million times!" She stops in front of me and yells in my face. Her breath hits me like small gusts of wind.

I fish the phone out of my pocket. "Oh, yeah. Battery's dead. Sorry, Mom."

My apology is not accepted. *Oh no.* She's full of rage. Her nostrils are dilated as if she's a dragon about to breathe fire. She yells, "Rachel, what the hell is wrong with you? You're nineteen years old! Do you know what I was doing when I was your age?"

I sure do, because she keeps reminding me. When she was my age, she already had me. She was a mom. I inhale deeply and try to keep calm because I don't want to get caught up in her drama.

"Mom, sorry I made you worry. I'm here now. And everything is fine. You can go back to watching your show."

"Don't you patronize me!" she screams. "You don't get to tell me what to do. It's the other way around. And I tell you to stop wasting your time in that stupid library and go to college!"

I'm so tired of this argument. We must have had it a hundred times before. "Mom—" I say, but she keeps at it.

"So your father and I got a divorce. So what? Half of

marriages end in divorce, and it's not the end of the world. It was two years ago—get over it already. Pull yourself together and think about your future!"

I can't take it anymore. "I did think about my future!" I yell and raise my hands. The sleeves fall to my elbows, and my scars are revealed.

That shuts her down. She falls back on the couch. Damn. I shouldn't have done that. Those scars are like nuclear explosive to her.

"Rach." Her voice is shaky. "Are you saying you have suicidal urges again?"

"No, Mom," I say with a softer tone. "I'm saying leave me alone. Let me be. I need to do things my own way, and I need time to figure things out."

She nods.

I think we're done. I'm heading to my room when she heats up again. "You're killing me, Rachel. You're just killing me with this attitude. Have you been working out?"

Where did that come from? "I just ran home from the library, does that count?"

"No. Rachel. The shrink said you need to work out regularly. Rachel! Don't leave while I'm talking to you!"

Bam. I go into my room and slam the door. She's impossible. I need to get the hell out of here. I wish I had enough money to rent my own place.

I plug the charger into my phone. I have twelve texts from my mother ranging from *"Call me"* to *"Where the hell are you, I'm going crazy over here."* There are no incoming texts from Chase. No missed calls. I have about twelve unanswered outgoing messages, though—the ones I sent him during the evening. They range from *"Call me"* to *"Where the hell are you, I'm going crazy over here."*

Huh.

One last try. I press Chase's number and this time he picks up. Well, someone picks up. There's no hello, but I can hear music.

"Chase? I'm going crazy. My mother is impossible!"

No one speaks. *Did someone steal his phone?* I look at the screen. *Did I call the wrong number?*

"Chase?" I ask again. "Are you there?"

"Oh, it's Nat. Chase's girlfriend. Chase is in the bathroom. Hang on."

Girlfriend? Since when does he have a girlfriend? A wave of painful jealousy crushes me like I got hit in my stomach. *I'm going to be sick.*

I hear her yelling his name and then—"Oh, here he comes. Chase, your phone. I think it's your baby sister. She said something about mother being impossible."

"What?" Chase says. "My mother died when I was fourteen. Give me that." After a moment of silence, he says, "It's not my sister, silly, it's Rachel." He talks to the phone, "Hi Rach, what's up?"

I'm too enraged to speak.

"Rachel? Are you alright?"

"You promised you'd help with the poetry night." my voice sounds like a little mouse squeaking.

"Oh. Right. That was tonight? Shoot. I forgot. Stop it, Nat!"

He says the last three words with a different tone, and I get it. He was preoccupied with his new girlfriend and didn't have time for me. The ex. The one who dumped him, and then forced him to be her best friend.

"Go to hell," I yell and hang up. I must have sounded like a three-year-old who's angry because she didn't get her cookie. He calls right back, but I don't pick up. I put the phone on silent.

I lie on the bedspread. This evening has been extremely emotional. I'd touched the top, and now I hit rock bottom.

When you go to enormous emotional heights, the fall feels much deeper. What's even worse is that the creative spark that's been burning inside me has been quenched.

Chase has a new girlfriend. For three years I held the title. Perhaps I would still own it if I hadn't broken up with him. *Love ends,* I remind myself. Love ends. My lungs are still contracted, but I can breathe a little easier.

So he has a new girlfriend. I should have expected that. Someone like Chase wouldn't stay single for long.

So he has a new girlfriend. Does that mean we can no longer be friends?

So he has a new girlfriend. Suddenly, I realize—I'm writing a poem. I grab my notebook and scribble down my thoughts.

So He Has a New Girlfriend writes itself. It's a complicated tale about a woman who finds out her ex has found a new love. And it ends with the line, *so he has a new girlfriend, and you're happy for him*.

On the second read-through, I realize the poem sucks. It's banal and meaningless. It's not even half as funny or smart as the poem Sarah recited tonight.

I reach into my pocket and pull out the folded paper I always carry with me. It's a poem titled *Rachel.* It captures the essence of who I am. I've carved it out of myself through blood and pain. I know *Rachel* by heart. But I still read it off the paper. I wish I could have the voice to stand up on stage and read it out loud.

ecca

MINUTES BEFORE MIDNIGHT, I'm exhausted. And sad. This day has drained me completely. I had such high expectations, and everything shattered to pieces. I'm lying in bed with the phone in my hand. I've been browsing through our photos, Lia's and mine. We look so happy. Smiling. I enlarge her smile and stare at the gap between her upper teeth. It's like a black hole that I gravitate towards.

I'm dozing off into a disturbing dream about gorillas when the phone vibrates. It's a text from Lia. *Finally.* I'm immediately awake and alert without any trace of fatigue.

Thanks for the food.

I'd redirected the veggie burgers to her place. It must have been waiting by the doorstep when she reached her apartment.

I reply with an emoji, the red heart. Lia sends me an emoji of a broken heart. Oh. That breaks *my* heart. So I send a smiley face, a clock, and a question mark. That's our private code for a video chat.

I put my earphones on, but it takes her forever to answer, and I've begun to drift into sleep when she finally calls. The vision is kind of blurry, but I can see her expression. She's squinting.

"How did it go with Rachel?"

"Terrible." I wipe my eyes. "It was just terrible." My voice is low. I don't want Rachel to hear me.

I don't know if it's the screen, but she looks paler. She puts her hands over her mouth, and I can hear her muffled voice as she says, "Oh no." She moves closer to the camera. "Baby, I'm so sorry I pushed you to do that." Her eyes are wide open, and it looks like she's in pain. "What did she say?"

I shake my head. "I didn't tell her. I mean, I was going to, but then we got into this huge fight. She was late."

"What do you mean, you didn't tell her? What did you fight about?"

"It's...I don't know. She was late, and I was worried. She didn't pick up her phone. One thing led to another. I told you, she's going through a phase."

Lia seems so disappointed.

"I'm sorry, baby. I was going to tell her. I promise I'll tell her the minute we patch things up, and then I'll tell the rest of the world." After a short pause, I add, "And I'm so sorry for tonight. I was selfish and stupid."

"Yes. You were." Her tone is harsh.

"Maybe I need to see a therapist to figure out why I subconsciously sabotage the most precious relationship I've ever had." Her face flexes a little. There's definitely a hint of a smile. But then her face stiffens again. It's like she's preparing herself to lift some weights.

"Listen, Becca, I don't have time for games. I've told you. I want to settle down."

"And I want to settle down too. I picture how it would be when we're both old and gray and still having sex." I touch her lips on my screen.

She smiles. "That's sweet, but I don't think you're ready to commit. You've never been with a woman before, and it's the first relationship you've had since your divorce. I'm thinking this whole thing might be just a rebound." Her lips shiver when she speaks.

I shake my head vigorously.

She continues. "Your daughter needs your full attention right now. Maybe this," she points at me and then at her, "maybe this has run its course. We had our fun. Maybe it's time to move on."

"Don't say that," I whisper. "I don't care that you're my first. Jason was my first, and we were together for eighteen years. I love you."

"Becca, be honest. Do you really love me? Or do you just love fucking me?"

The thought of fucking her makes my breath shorter. I close my eyes. How I love to stick my tongue into her folds and lick her slowly, inch by inch, like an archaeologist exposing a rare find.

"Oh baby," she says, her voice husky. "I love fucking you too. You're so delicious. You're so pretty when you come."

I slide my hand down my pajama pants. I move the phone down, so she can see what I'm doing. We've been having phone sex for quite a while now, so we have a routine. This is how it always starts.

"Oh yeah." She's excited. "Let me see your little clit. I want to say hi."

I slide the phone down my pants. I can still hear her talking in my earphones.

"Hello there, lovely," Lia says, "It was nice knowing you. Guess it's time to say goodbye now."

I lift the phone back up to my face. "What? Lia, no! It's not just fucking. I love you, baby. I love everything about you. I love your smell. And your voice. I just love the sound of your voice. I don't care what you say. I could listen to you for hours. And I love the way you care about your trainees. You're my angel. Baby, sorry, I know you hate it when I call you angel. Please don't leave me. Please. I'll die without you."

She's quiet for a long time.

Did we lose our connection? "Lia?" I whisper. "Are you there?"

"Becca." She whispers too. "I feel like we have something real. It's rare to feel so deeply connected after only a few short months."

I nod. Salty tears fill my mouth. I don't bother to wipe them. This is too intense.

"I don't want to get hurt again, Becca. And I know you're going to break my heart."

I shake my head. "No. No."

She looks away from the screen for a second. "Why are you so afraid to tell Rachel, anyway? Can you at least tell me that? I know you're not being honest with me, and I want to know the truth."

Telling the truth means betraying Rachel's trust. I take a deep breath. There's no way around it. I must do it, or I'll lose Lia. I hope that Rachel will forgive me. "Rachel didn't react well when her father and I got divorced."

"What do you mean? Wasn't she like, seventeen?"

"Yeah." I nod. "She was overwhelmed by the fact that Jason fell in love with someone else. We weren't unhappy, Jason and I. We had a normal middle-class life. So it was a shock to her. She couldn't figure it out. Renee was his assistant for years before it happened. Before they fell in love."

I pause for a second and close my eyes. I don't like to revisit these memories.

"We sat down with her, Jason and I, and told her we were separating. Explained the whole thing. We let her choose where she wanted to stay, told her we loved her and would always love her."

"You did it by the book," Lia says, and I nod.

"A day later, she broke up with her boyfriend. One day she adored Chase. He was The One. And the next, she dumps him on a whim. They were a power couple, had been going on strong for two and a half years. They had bright futures ahead of them. Both had gotten accepted to U of C, and they were so proud and excited. It was their plan to go to college together." I pause. Lia looks invested in the story. "But then her grades began dropping. She'd been a straight-A student since kindergarten. Suddenly, education wasn't important anymore." I twitch my face. "It's not easy to relive those painful times." I didn't realize how profoundly sad she was. As it happened, I was also sad at the time. So I missed all the clues," my voice gets shaky, "It took me almost a year to figure out what was going on with her."

I pause for a minute, not sure how to continue. I take a breath. "Then one day, I get home from work, and she's in the bathroom." I choke. I can't speak. I show Lia my wrists, pass my fingers over them.

Lia understands. She puts her hands over her mouth. Her eyes are wide open.

It takes me a while to stop shaking. I don't tell her what Rachel said. That she didn't want to die, that it was just an experiment. "What did you want to achieve?" I'd asked, but she'd said I wouldn't understand. She'd asked me to let it go, to keep it between us and never tell a living soul. I swore.

"She goes to a therapist now. I think she's doing better,

but I don't know." I shrug. "Some days are better than others. Today wasn't one of them."

Lia reaches her hand out toward the camera.

"Bexy. Bex. I'm so sorry, honey."

I nod. "I've never told anyone about—" I expose my wrists again. "Not even Jason. Rachel made me swear. I'm betraying her trust now, so…"

Lia waits for me to get a grip. "Baby, I'm so moved you chose to share this with me." She hesitates for a minute. "But you clearly need to concentrate on her right now. I get it."

I sob. I know where she's going with this.

"I have real feelings for you, Bex, but I think we need to take a break."

achel

THERE'S a line of people standing outside the cafe where Sarah wanted to meet me. I hate lines, and I hate this one in particular. It's so stupid. There are three other cafes in close vicinity, yet people are flocking tothis one as if it's giving away free coffee, which is quite the contrary. The coffee here is pricey, and after I get a chance to taste it, I can also say it's yuck.

Sarah's working behind the counter. I see her when the line progresses and I'm finally inside the cafe. Her hair is pink but other than that she looks the same, with those piercing green eyes and pretty smile. She gives me a wave when she sees me waiting in line. People standing in front of me turn back to see who she is waving at. *So embarrassing.* I pull my hoodie over my head. That makes me feel a little bit better.

I slide into an empty booth with my crappy latte and watch the crowd. It's fascinating.

Sarah announces, "Paul, tall double-latte, boiled Turkish." A bearded guy with a man bun and an expensive-looking suit hurries toward the counter and grabs his drink. A young woman, probably someone's personal assistant, orders eight different drinks, and the people standing behind her bitch bitterly.

One of them, a short, chubby young man yells, "Open a different fucking line for coffee runs, damn it." Some of the people standing next to him nod with agreement. Others don't seem to care, their noses stuck in their phones. I guess it's a daily routine for most of them, but as an outside observer, the whole scene looks surreal.

I take out my notebook and start writing. It's not really a poem, just some general reflections about the situation, like, *the smell of coffee in the morning is the smell of capitalism.* Or *double orange, please is a ginger lady having pumpkin latte.* I sit and write and watch the line get shorter and thinner and then, poof, it ends. Just like that.

The only people who are at the cafe now, besides the servers, are working on laptops, looking very serious. Sarah slides into the seat facing me. She's holding two steaming paper mugs. I close my notebook quickly and put it in my backpack.

"Tea," she says and shifts a mug toward me. "Funnily enough, the tea here is much better than the coffee." She chuckles. I don't know how to react. The right thing would probably be to smile and nod, but my face freezes when I try to put on a smile. It's so odd.

"It's herbal," she says. "Lemon and tangerine." She slurps from hers then spits the liquid back into the mug. "Too hot," she cries. "Burnt my mouth." She runs back to the counter, and when she returns, there's an ice cube in her mouth. She moves it from side to side like bubblegum then spits it into the mug.

I'm enchanted and disgusted at the same time. I don't know what to say, and even if I did, I definitely wouldn't say it. She's heard my voice.

I look at my phone. It's 9:05 a.m. I've been sitting in the booth for forty minutes. I wonder why she asked to meet at half-past eight, knowing she would be busy with the morning rush.

Sarah says, "I picture the people who come here each morning to get their coffee dose. Now they're sitting in their little cubicles, hammering away on their little computers." She mimics them by typing quickly on the table. "I pity them, you know? It might be that this one cup of coffee they get here every morning is the only moment of joy they have throughout their day. It makes me sad." She sips from her tea and then sighs with content. Obviously, her beverage is now the right temperature.

I would be miserable working in an office, but not everyone is like me. My mother is happy working nine to five. Well, most of the time. I don't say anything though. There's the issue of my voice. It's easier to remain quiet and just nod as if I agree.

The silence between us deepens. I point at her hair and say, "Pink."

She combs her fingers through the crest. "Oh yeah," she says. "You're very observant about hair, aren't you?"

I blush.

She smiles and touches my hand. "Just kidding. Don't mean to offend you. You're a sweet girl. Anyway, I was in the mood for pink this morning. You know, like a fairy. I'm the coffee fairy." She laughs. It's a rough laugh.

I'm too shy to look at her, and I divert my eyes the other way. The counter is empty now, the servers on their break. Some of them are smoking outside by the curb. A big black guy sits at the far corner, having a drink and doing a crossword puzzle. I'm not sure if he's a customer or a barista.

I don't know why I'm too embarrassed to look directly at Sarah.

"So, Rachel, what were you doodling in your little notebook?"

I flush.

"Can I have a look?" She smiles. She looks genuinely interested. I take my notebook out, hesitate for a moment, then give it to her. As I do, my sleeve slides up and shows the scar on my wrist. She notices it; I can see it in her microexpressions. But she doesn't say anything.

No one has ever read my poems. I'm so nervous, I sit on

my sweaty palms and shift from side to side on the vinyl cushion. It makes farting noises, which makes me flush again.

She nods as she reads. And then she chuckles. "That's good," she says. Her eyes meet mine. They're sparkling with joy. She points to a specific line. I look down. Her fingernails are bitten to the quick. Just like mine.

She reads, "A Turkish café, made from Columbian beans, pressed in an Italian machine, and served to an Asian woman in the suburbs of Chicago. That's cultural fusion in one cup."

Her eyes sparkle when she looks at me. They're so clear, they're like the crystal pond in my happy place. It's where I go when I feel depressed, a place that exists only in my dreams. In my fantasy, I float on my back in the warm water. The currents carry me softly, and I feel completely safe, guarded. That's how I feel when I look into Sarah's eyes.

"You're such a raw talent," she says. She leans over and grabs my arm. "Why didn't you read at the event?"

I shrug. I can't tell her that I hate my voice because, *duh.*

"I thought that was the whole point of the event. I mean, if I were you, I would have planned the whole thing only so I could read." She grins.

"How do you know I planned it?" I'm so intrigued, I can't keep quiet.

She raises her eyebrows and pauses for a minute. "I did my research."

What does that mean? Who? How? Is that what Mrs. Ilman whispered in her ear?

I have so many questions. I wish she would elaborate, but she doesn't say anything. Is she waiting for me to ask?

She slurps her tea. I sip mine too. Carefully, though. Mine is still hot.

"Fine," she says with a sigh. "You can stop with the begging. I'll just tell you."

I smile.

"I used to work at the library when I was your age. Gosh, that was almost a decade ago. Mrs. Ilman had just been promoted to head librarian. She speaks very highly of you, by the way. Mrs. Ilman, that is. She said you're a young prodigy, and I should do you no harm. That's what she whispered in my ear the other day, in case you were wondering." My smile widens. Her smile is crooked.

"She's not very subtle, our Mrs. Ilman, is she?" Sarah leans forward over the table, "Knowing how narrow-minded and cheap this woman is, I guess it takes a bulldozer to make Mrs. Ilman do something out of her comfort zone. And a Spoken Word event is way out of it, as I recall." I nod in agreement. She is correct. "So, I came over with the sole purpose of meeting that bulldozer. Imagine my surprise when I find out it's a fragile nineteen-year-old that's afraid to speak." She looks at me.

I flush. She's very direct. I like it. I like her. I want to be direct, candid, and blunt like her.

"I hate my voice." I look down. It's the first time I've admitted that to someone who's not my family. Or my therapist. Of course, they all say my voice is perfectly alright. That's what they're supposed to say, right? They love me, and they want to comfort me and convince me there's nothing wrong with me, and it's stupid because everything they say is neither comforting nor convincing.

If she tells me my voice is fine, I'll just get up and leave without saying anything. That would be a direct and blunt act. In fact, it would be poetic.

She laughs. "Dear, I think you've gotten it all wrong. In the Spoken Word world, having a funny voice is a big advantage. And when I say big, I mean huge. It's going to be your signature. People are going to come *specifically* to hear you speak. I wish I had a voice like yours."

I didn't expect that. I look up into her eyes. They're

limpid and bright, like the sky. She's not bullshitting me. She really means it. But I still have to ask. "Really?"

"Darling, I would never ever in a million years, Scout's honor," she lifts three fingers in a Scout's swear, "say something I don't think to be true." She looks dead serious. "Life's too short. I don't have the time to say all the meaningful things I want to say, so lies and make-believe? Unh-uh. I don't have time for that."

"That's exactly what I think. Only you say it better."

She smiles. "Well, I'm older. It took me years to refine that thought. But it'll be easier for you— You can borrow mine." She laughs that bitter laugh again. It sounds somewhat vulgar. "Hell, that's what I did when I started out. We poets always get inspired by the generation that came before us."

She pauses to take a long sip from her mug. "Rachel, whatever-your-last-name is, it would be a privilege to be your mentor."

Only then do I realize that this meeting was an interview. And I was accepted.

CHAPTER 4

achel

"THIS CAFE WOULD BE OUR HEADQUARTERS," Sarah says. "We'll meet here for two hours, once a week, when our shifts allow. We'll analyze your work, and I'll give you homework which you'll do to the T. Understood?"

"I don't have any money—"

She raises her hand and stops me mid-sentence. "I don't want money. All I want is your commitment to be my mentee. And by that, I mean for you to put your heart and soul into this. I can see you have the potential to become a great poet, but you need to invest the time and look bravely inside yourself. Are you willing to do that?"

Of course I'm willing. I've cut myself in order to bleed out my poetry. But I don't say that. I try to hide my enthusiasm, but it's hard. Her speech was flattering and motivating, but I've learned to be suspicious of things that are too good to be true, things that fall into my lap without me making an effort to get them. Things like love.

"What's in it for you?"

She frowns. "It's complicated."

"You're a poet, aren't you? Dig deep inside you and tell me what's what."

She laughs that vulgar laugh. "Touché, Ms. Rachel. I see you've got fire in you. That's great."

I'm not letting her slide that easy.

"Fine, Jesus," she finally says. Her voice is tough, but her eyes are smiling. "I had a mentor when I started my journey, and now it's my turn to give back."

It's a great answer, and I feel it might be part of the truth, but there's more to it. So I wait. Quietly. It's easy for me. I'm used to not speaking.

"Mentoring is a two-way street, Rachel. I expect to learn from you too."

"What can I teach you?" I chuckle. "I know nothing. I barely graduated high school."

"You don't need a diploma to be a poet, silly."

"Tell that to my mother. She thinks you need to have a college education for everything.

"Well, there's some truth to that. Studying English can never hurt. Poetry is a hard nut to crack on your own."

"Do you have a college degree?"

"Yeah. I have an MFA."

I unzip and re-zip my hoodie. Her eyes are punching me.

"Seriously, Rachel. Every mentor is also a mentee. It's a matter of perspective and openness. And I'm open. To anything. To everything. Are you?"

I nod in agreement. *But am I really?* I recall how Sarah rhymed about her sexual extravaganza at the Spoken Word event, and I wonder, does she want me to make another verse in her poem?

"Oh, relax," she says as if she read my mind, "I took some literary freedom in that poem. We're allowed to do it, you know. We don't have to tell the truth, even when we write in the first person." She chuckles. "And the truth is, I've never turned anybody who didn't want to be turned in the first place."

Do I want to be turned?

"OK, fine," she says after a short pause. "I'm suffering from a terrible writer's block. It's been going on for months now, ever since I was listed in that 30 under 30 list. It closed my creativity."

"I'm so sorry."

She waves her hand in dismissal. "I've tried meditations. I've tried drugs. Cleanses. Morning papers. I've tried it all, and nothing helps." She chuckles. It's a dry laugh. "I couldn't even produce something decent for my niece's third birthday. So, I'm thinking that helping someone who's just starting out will help me get my mojo back." She bites on her bitten-down fingernails.

I can feel the pain in her voice. And I totally identify. "Fine. I'll do it. I'll be your mentee."

She grins hesitantly. "Do you commit to doing everything I say?"

"To the T." I sit on my hands to stop them from sweating. I hope she won't ask me to shake hands to close our deal, which of course she does. Her hands are sweaty as well.

"So, listen," Sarah says. "Your first assignment. I want you to get a thesaurus. It's a poet's best friend. I know there are plenty of online dictionaries now, but I want you to get a real one. You should keep it by your side all the time. Seriously. Always. Whenever you have a minute, just look up some random words. It works on a subconscious level—it's amazing. You won't believe how good your linguistic skills get in no time at all."

She hugs me before I leave, and there's that lavender and lilies smell again. I inhale it. I want to keep it in my nose for a while; it's full of inspiration.

~

THERE'S an old thesaurus in the language section at the library amongst some heavy dictionaries. It looks like it's been ages since it was checked out, which is understandable —nowadays you can have entire encyclopedias on your phone.

It's funny to realize that the last person to borrow the thesaurus was Sarah Walters. Her old picture appears in the system when I check out the book. She looks so plain with her brown hair gathered into a ponytail. Her eyes pierce me through the screen. She looks so much better now.

Mrs. Ilman catches me staring at her picture and scoffs. "I got complaints, just so you know, about this one." She nods her head toward the screen. "Foul language, inappropriate subjects." She clicks her tongue and shakes her head in self-righteousness.

I guess she means complaints about Sarah's performance at the Spoken Word event. Her poem was indeed full of profanities.

Mrs. Ilman points at me. "She's trouble, Sarah Walters. I knew it then, and I know it now. Stay away from her, Rachel. Good girls like you should not hang out with scum."

"Yes, Mrs. Ilman." I try to keep my face straight. Sarah and I would have a laugh about it at our next meeting.

"Caught her by the 200s," Mrs. Ilman leans over and whispers thunderously into my ear. "The *religious* section," she clarifies.

Probably my face gave away the fact that I don't know the Dewey system by heart as she does.

She leans even closer. Her eyebrows are pulled together. "She was kissing a girl." Mrs. Ilman shivers as someone would after seeing a corpse. "Imagine that. Kissing a girl in the Bible section. The nerve of her!" She clicks her tongue. "Don't you smile at me, Rachel Davis. I'm not narrow-minded. I know these things exist. But you don't go around doing them in public libraries."

"Yes, Mrs. Ilman," I say. My voice is higher pitched than normal, but she doesn't seem to notice. I guess it's the first time my voice has saved me, and that is truly something to rejoice about.

Mrs. Ilman examines me. Her eyes are like little black slits. "There's something about you. I can't put my finger on it. You're not as pretty as her, not with those eyes, of course. But you do have your youth on your side." She's grumbling. I don't know if I should be offended or flattered.

"Mrs. Ilman?"

She straightens her starched, white, button-down blouse and clears her throat. "I can't ask you directly because that would be considered personal, and what you do in your own private time is your business, but I sure hope I will not find you kissing a girl in the religion section, or any other section, for that matter, of my library. Please, spare me. I have not yet recovered from the previous incident."

"Yes, Mrs. Ilman," I say. I wonder, *what makes her think I'm attracted to girls?*

ecca

I DEVOTE MYSELF TO WORK. Every waking moment is agonizing with the pain of yearning for my loved one. I work sixty hours a week, and that makes my clients very happy because their reports get done super-fast. It makes my colleagues super-happy because I'm fine with doing the heavy-lifting for everyone. And of course, my boss, Darren, is ecstatic about it. He gets the additional work without the need to pay extra. Everyone is happy but me. I'm tired and grumpy, and I eat too much. My mood swings between self-pity and guilt. One minute I think, *why do I deserve this?* And the next, I whip myself mentally, saying, *of course you deserve it. It's your fault. Look at yourself, fat and ugly and boring. You can't keep up with someone as magnificent as Lia. No matter what you do, you'll never be in her league.*

At night, I fall into a deep, dreamless sleep, which is a blessing. And every morning, I wake up with a shred of optimism. I tell myself, *this is just a temporary break. I'm certain she'll call today and say she misses me and wants to meet.*

On the way to work, I look for signs to reinforce my positivity. If one of Rhianna's songs plays on KissFM in the morning, that's a good sign. If the rain stops when I get to the parking lot, it's another good sign. If Lucy at reception remembers to bring me my favorite soy latte, that's the best sign of all. It means Lia's definitely going to call me today.

I have an elaborate fantasy about it. She says, "Hey Bexy, I miss you so much, and I reply, "Baby, I miss you too." And her throat will be choked up when she says she made a terrible mistake, and she can't live without me.

Signs pile up throughout the day. Darren tells me a joke

as he passes by my office. That's a huge one. I get a thank you note from Shirley for helping her figure out the new software. But Lia doesn't call, and as the day progresses, I get depressed and anxious. I find myself wandering to the kitchenette and having way too many donuts, which doesn't fill the deep hole inside me. And as another evening approaches without a word from Lia, I know this break actually means breakup.

Three weeks into our breakup, I still can't get her out of my mind. My heart misses a beat whenever I hear a voice similar to hers, or when someone says a word that starts with a *Li* like liaison, which is a common word around the office. Each time, I straighten up in my seat only to be disappointed again when the *Li* turns to be 'listen' or 'leeway,' which is another common word in my line of work.

On the outside, I'm the perfectly reasonable Becca, senior CPA. Well, I hope that's how my colleagues see me. Inside, I'm a mixture of sadness and anger.

Sometimes I can't hold back my tears, which seem to burst free at the most inconvenient moments, like during a Monday morning brief. I have to excuse myself quickly before I become the talk of the day. I run outside and hide in my car until my face is presentable again.

Other times, I lash out with disproportionate reactions, like this morning when I yelled at Darren in front of the whole office because he made a tiny mistake in his calculations. He stormed out and went directly to HR, demanding to fire me. I had to do damage control and apologize to the entire personnel. Then Sheila calls me in, and I know I'll have to reassure her she didn't make a fatal mistake by promoting me to be her successor.

I go to the bathroom to brace myself for the meeting. And as I lean down to wash my face, I catch my reflection in the mirror. I have a crazy look in my eyes like the one Rachel had in her eyes that horrible day.

The water keeps pouring while I stare at my reflection, mesmerized. I'm so focused on my face that I don't hear when Sheila enters. I don't know how long she's been standing behind me. Watching me. Oh god. Did I look at Rachel the same way she looks at me? I see compassion in her eyes but also fear.

She steps forward and turns off the faucet then makes eye contact via the mirror.

"Becca, are you OK?" Her voice is soft.

I nod. Because I can't tell her that yesterday after work, I parked by the gym for two consecutive hours in the vain hope that Lia would come out to me.

"How's Rachel doing?"

"She's fine," I say. My voice cracks.

Sheila touches my forearm. "Becca, dear, we've known each other for a very long time now, so please forgive me for invading your privacy. It's only because I'm truly worried about you, dear. You need to take better care of yourself."

It's a very polite and indirect way to say I've gained weight. I thank her coldly.

"You've been working like crazy lately; why don't you take a few days to rest? Maybe a relaxing weekend at a spa? My treat."

Yeah. As if rest would help my issues. I scoff and kindly decline her generous offer. Still, she makes me take the rest of the day off.

As I step out, I feel Lucy's, the receptionist, eyes piercing my back.

CHAPTER 5

achel

"Darling, darling, Rachel," Sarah says. This time her hair is plain brown, her crest flattened with gel and bobby pins. She looks a lot like that plain photo from her old library card.

It's the end of the morning rush, and she looks tired, somewhat beaten up from life. She releases a sigh as she sits at our regular booth. Poet Corner, we call it.

"I've got to tell you, my young protégé, this is a poet's life in its glory." Her gesture covers the cafe. There are spills on the floor. The tables are dirty. The trash cans are full. She sounds bitter.

I look at her fiercely until I capture her gaze. I shrug. *So what?* My eyes say everything. It is what it is. She smiles.

"I must warn you, young Rachel, being a poet means a life of struggle. You won't be able to afford nice things. You'll have to live with a roommate even when you're approaching thirty. And you'll want to scream when you hear her fuck her fucking boyfriend all night long, and you have to wake up at fucking five a.m. and go to your shitty morning shift at a shitty cafe. Maybe I'm not the right person to be your mentor."

She spreads her hands on the table and lays her head on them. She closes her eyes.

I let her rest for a while. "If you could go back, would you do things differently?"

She straightens up and smiles. "Huh," she says and taps on my arm. "I knew I picked a smart one." She pauses for a second. "To answer your question, no. I wouldn't."

"My mom, I told you about her, she's pushing me to go to college. She's a certified CPA. She thinks I should follow in her footsteps. I was always good at math. But I'm horrified at the thought of doing that all my life. Working nine to five in an office. It's so…" I look for the right words.

"Boring?" Sarah suggests.

I shake my head. "Meaningless."

She nods in agreement. "Well, Rachel, I think this is the longest I've ever heard you speak, and I can tell you that, when you do talk, you say important stuff. I like you, Rachel Davis, I like you a lot."

I flush. *And I like you too, Sarah Walters.* I say it in my heart. I can't stop thinking about her. When we part, I wait impatiently for our next meeting. I live for these sessions.

ecca

RACHEL'S SITTING at the kitchen table. She looks surprised to see me home and hurries to gather her stuff. I grit my teeth. She's been giving me the silent treatment ever since the night of our fight.

"Hello," I say coldly. I open the fridge, looking for a sweet, comforting treat.

"Mom, what are you doing home so early?"

"I could ask you the same thing." I grab a spoon for my chocolate pudding and sit down next to her.

I expect her to leave, but she stays, holding her stuff on her knees. I'm curious about the top-secret project she's been working on, but I don't ask. What's the point? I'm not going to get an honest answer.

"Seriously, Mom, what's going on with you? You've been in this rotten mood since, like, forever."

"Three weeks and five days, to be precise."

She gasps and looks away. I give her a good look. She looks so pretty. Her eyes are sparkling. She seems…in love. The realization makes me drop a spoonful of pudding on the table. Is that it? But with who? Is it someone new? Did she meet someone at the library? I try to jog my memory. Whenever she bothers to talk about her work, she just bitches about that head librarian, Mrs. Ilman. She never mentions boys. Well, except Chase. Curiosity consumes me. Are they back together?

"You seem happy," I say.

She lowers her eyes. Huh. I hit a nerve. My chocolate pudding is done. I go back to the fridge. It's time for those pizza leftovers. "How's work?" I ask. I expect a shrug as an answer. Recently, that's all I get.

"Fine. I took a day off."

"Any plans?"

She flushes again. "I have a thing."

"A thing?"

She changes the subject before I have a chance to dig deeper. "Why are you home so early?"

"I do such a good job, Sheila gave me the afternoon off," I reply with my mouth full. It's close enough to the truth. And after all, I am extremely good at my work.

We sit quietly for a second. I chew quickly, guessing it's my turn to ask her something now. She looks at me bingeing away. It's not a pretty sight.

"Mom. Why aren't you working out anymore?"

I gasp and choke on a piece of pizza. She pours me a glass of water, and I cough for a good two minutes before I catch my breath.

"Well, if my memory serves me right, the only reason I went into that endeavor in the first place was because of you, Rachel Davis. And as I recall, the therapist specifically prescribed working out for you." My tone is blaming. Too blaming. Damn. Now I blame myself.

"I run, Mom. I already told you."

"I know, I know. You run with Chase. At the U of C." I'm asking, but somehow it comes out as a statement.

She flushes again, and I guess they never even leave the dorms. Which is great. They're nineteen. They should fuck like crazy. Her reaction is such a relief. She's normal. Pffff.

"Mom." Rachel waits for my eyes to meet hers. "I'm sorry for being such an ass."

"I'm sorry too, Rach. I didn't mean to yell."

She opens her mouth, and I can see she wants to say something. She struggles to find the right words.

"Sorry for saying that awful thing about killing myself. I didn't mean it."

I nod. That's not what she wanted to say. I can feel it. I wait. But she's done. She's walking away.

"Rach," I call after her. "Are you all right? I worry. You know how I am. I just want to know if you're fine."

She grins and nods enthusiastically. "I'm great, Mom. The best I've ever been." She rushes back and kisses me on my cheek. "I love you, Mom."

"Love you too."

She goes to her room, and I sit at the table for a long time, looking at the thin air where she stood just minutes ago. I'm not touching the pizza. It's gone cold, but I've eaten colder over these last three weeks and five days.

"Huh." I finally say. I shake my head and chuckle. It's a bitter laugh. She's finally over her phase. If only she'd gotten out of it three weeks and five days ago, my life would be completely different.

CHAPTER 6

ecca

ONLY WHEN RACHEL leaves for her thing I'm motivated enough to get up from the kitchen table where I've been sitting and grieving for who-knows-how-long. The chair is sticky, and it's hard to get up. I feel like the entire universe is weighing me down in an effort to stop my relationship with Lia. It's frightening because every bone in my body is telling me this was meant to be. The noise the chair makes as I get up sounds like the universe mocking me. Who am I to challenge the universe?

Seeing Rachel cheered up, vital, and energetic moves something in me.

All my feelings push me to pick up the phone and sign up for one of Lia's classes. Advanced Step Aerobics, to be precise. At 6 p.m. I'm not even remotely advanced, but it was the only class with an open spot. I know this class is going to be painful on so many levels, but at least it'll give me a chance to see her. *One good look at her, and I'll know if we still have a chance.*

It takes me two hours to get ready. It's not just about being pretty. My appearance should send a message. So, I'm wearing the sweats I wore the first time we met. I fix my hair the same way. Only this time, my eyes aren't puffy, and I'm wearing the red-hot lipstick Lia loves.

The class is swarming with new faces. Energy levels are high. I find a spot at the back of the room and look for Lia in the crowd. Although she's tiny, I spot her almost immediately. She's standing by the mirror and chatting with a fit blonde woman wearing a neon-green outfit. Then I catch my reflection, and I compare myself to this blonde lady. There are silver lines in my hair and lumps of flab on my torso and thighs. My heart sinks. I can't compete.

Lia notices me, and she flinches for a fraction of a second before she pulls herself together. I wave and smile. No use. She avoids making eye contact. *Damn.* The blonde looks at her with adoring eyes while she speaks. I can't hear the words, but I see the gestures and the body language. She's excited, and I can't blame her. Who wouldn't be excited, talking to such a goddess? Lia pulls her hair up, and the blonde imitates her. It's a statement. They're two peas in one pod. I should gather my stuff and leave. Clearly, I've been replaced. But the class starts, and I know how Lia hates people who leave in the middle. I follow her instructions like a zombie.

She's killing us. Jumping jacks and mambos and running in place. Two minutes in, and I'm dripping sweat like a galloping horse. The pretty blonde, who stands in the first line, keeps smiling. There are no sweat beads on her forehead. She doesn't take her eyes off Lia.

"What's gotten into her today?" whispers a man who's

standing next to me when we both take a break to catch our breath.

I shrug. "Maybe she's in love," I say. My voice cracks.

Lia is standing with her back to us, now doing squats. One leg on the step, the other on the floor. She makes eye contact with me via the mirror and yells, "You two ladies in the back! Would you like to have a coffee with your chit-chat?" She pouts. My heart misses a beat. I love her so much.

The blonde laughs hysterically.

The guy gives me a look and chuckles. I smile back at him, thinking, *well, at least I got her attention.*

"Is she always such a bitch?" he whispers.

"She is," I say and touch his arm. I smile and flutter my eyelashes. I hope she sees me flirting with him.

"Well, her looks make up for her bitchiness," he says. She *is* eye candy with her red-hot sports bra and micro skirt.

I laugh as if he just told the funniest joke in the history of jokes. "Don't go there, dude, she's not into men," I whisper.

He chuckles. "Well, that gives me something else to think about, huh?" He winks at me.

"You two at the back," Lia roars. "Get a room already!"

Everybody laughs.

"Lia, you're hilarious!" says the blonde. She's such a fake. How come Lia doesn't see that?

I linger when the class ends. People always go to thank Lia and chat. They want to share their experience. I wait for them to disperse. The blonde lingers too. She stands by Lia, and at one point, Lia grabs her arm. The blonde's face lights up.

Damn. Lia has clearly moved on. Tears blur my vision. I need to leave, ASAP. I throw my stuff into my bag and head for the door. *Damn. Damn. Damn.* The tears come pouring down.

"Hey." Someone taps my shoulder. "Would you like to get

a drink?" It's the guy from earlier. He notices my tears and raises his brows. "Oh, what's wrong, honey? Is it something I did?"

I shake my head. I can't speak. He holds me, trying to comfort me. And I'm so embarrassed. So out of place.

Suddenly, Lia storms over. She pulls me out of his arms. "You're Zach, right?"

He nods.

"Well, Zach, take your filthy hands off her. This one's mine." She's all fiery.

He's taller. And wider. But she's scarier. He takes two steps back and raises his arms, giving in.

"Becca, would you please step into my office?" She pushes me into the equipment closet and shuts the door behind us. I stumble over a pile of blue physio balls and fall on my back. Lia jumps on top of me like we're in a ball pit. She crushes her lips to mine.

I totally didn't see that coming. It's an angry kiss. Her lips are harsh, brutalizing mine. But I'm happy. A kiss is a kiss. The feel of her skin on my skin is intoxicating. I inhale her unique aroma. Her hands travel all over my body, and she doesn't need to say it; I can feel in her touch how much she misses me.

I want to wrap my hands around her, but I have to hold on to the shaky surface underneath. I manage to put one hand on her cheek and caress her. Her kiss softens as she opens her mouth wider, and I can feel the tip of her tongue probing, searching for mine.

She groans as the kiss deepens. Our lips are fused together once again, and, for a short moment of bliss, I forget everything and everyone. There is just me and her and no one else in the entire universe. I don't mind that we're locked in a filthy equipment closet. All I care about is her touch.

She stops abruptly and rips her lips from mine. My lips

hurt as if they are bruised. It's a good pain, like sore muscles after physical activity. I reach my hand to her neck and try to pull her down toward me.

"No," she says and jumps to her feet.

"Lia," I whisper. Saying her name is such a joy. With her hands on her waist, she's towering over me, and that's certainly a first. She gives me one of her fiery looks.

"How dare you," she mutters through her teeth. "How dare you come to my workplace and flirt in front of my eyes? Have you no shame?"

"Lia," I say as I struggle to get up.

"Don't you 'Lia' me. There's no excuse for what you did."

"Let me explain—"

"No!"

I finally find my balance, but she pushes me back down and storms out. We're done. Absolutely, totally done.

A shred of light sneaks underneath the closet door until somebody turns it out. Was it Lia?

I'm alone in the dark. *Well, now you know.* I lie there for a while. My eyes get used to the dark, but my mind doesn't. I force myself to get up. To get out.

It takes enormous willpower to get back to the car. To drive home.

I text Sheila, telling her I'm going to take her advice and take a few days off.

And that few days turns into two weeks.

achel

"Show me something. One of your latest works," Sarah says. It's our fourth meeting and this is the first time she has asked to read one of my poems.

I turn the pages of my notebook. I don't have anything good. I stop when I reach that lame piece of writing titled *So You Have a New Girlfriend* I wrote after the Spoken Word event. As I browse the short lines, I think about my *Rachel* poem, tucked away in my pocket. I'm not ready to show her that.

"You don't need to find a perfect example," Sarah says. "May I?" She doesn't wait for an answer and gently turns the notebook toward her.

"Okay," she says after she reads the poem. "It's a good first draft. Now we need to revise. Make it sharper and add layers to it so that a reader will discover something new with each read. What were you thinking when you wrote it?"

I shrug. "I don't know."

"Come on, you need to be brave and honest, or this, all this," she gestures with her hands between us, "won't work.

I inhale deeply.

"I had this boyfriend. Chase. We were together since sophomore year and broke up two months before graduation, but we stayed friends. I mean, like best friends. I wrote this poem when I found out he'd moved on. He has a new girlfriend now. Her name is Nat." I say the name with disgust.

"OK," Sarah says contemplatively. "I hear a lot of emotions here. Your poem should reflect that. Let's start with that. Emotional connection."

We work for two hours. I like the result. It's much better, but it's not perfect.

Sarah yawns and stretches her hands. "If you ask me, I think this boy is a fool for dumping you. You're such a catch, Rach."

"It was the other way around," I whisper.

"You broke up with him?" She raises her eyebrows.

I nod.

"But why? You clearly had a connection."

I shrug. "Love ends."

She stares at me, waiting for me to elaborate.

"I wanted to end it sooner rather than later. Before I got too involved. I didn't want to get hurt."

Sarah grabs my hands; there are tears in her eyes. "Darling, getting hurt is part of our human experience. You can't escape that."

I nod. She's right, of course. Her life perspective blows my mind.

"As a poet, you harvest pain and make it an inspiration. Don't run away from hurt, Rachel. You need to be authentic. Stand tall and take what's coming, the good and the bad."

I shiver. My hands are already stretched out on the table. Slowly, I roll up my sleeves. I know she's gotten a glimpse of my scars before, but not like this. Not up front in her face. As I'm putting them on the table, I think that would be a great title for a poem. *Putting My Scars On The Table.*

I don't say anything. Sarah isn't talking either. She looks at me. Then she lays her hands on the table and rolls her sleeves up. Way up. Her arms are full of cuts.

There's no need for words. We share the sisterhood of the knife.

We hold hands and stare at each other. We share so many similarities. It's like we're soulmates.

~

MRS. ILMAN CONSULTS the Bible whenever she needs to make an important decision. She opens it on a random page and always finds an answer to her specific dilemma on that specific page. I decide to use the same method with my thesaurus.

On the bus ride, I take it out of my backpack and open it to a random page. Rotten. Worse than bad. Decayed.

"Hi, Rach," a familiar voice says.

"Chase." He looks good. His long hair is brushed back, and the sides are cut short. He has a beard now, and he's wearing fashionable hipster clothes. I sense there's a guiding female hand in this new style. He slides into the seat next to me.

"You're reading the dictionary now?" His eyes glisten mischievously as he looks at my book. He acts as if we're still friends. "That's alright, the weird look is quite becoming on you," he teases.

I close the book abruptly and give him a shove with my shoulder. "And what do I call your look? Nat?" It's not easy to roll her name on my tongue, although it's just the one syllable.

He shrugs. Not from embarrassment, but from modesty. It's like he's proud she dresses him. "She's an art major, so…"

I nod. He tries to cross his legs, but the jeans he's wearing are too skinny. It doesn't seem to bother him. When we were together, he didn't want to be restricted by items of clothing. Guess he changed his mind about that too.

"So, how's life? You still work at the library?"

"No. They fired me after the Spoken Word event. Because I failed to bring in a host."

"Oh, Rach, I'm so sorry!" He looks stricken. "I'll call and tell them it's my fault. Damn. I feel so bad now."

I let him loiter in his guilt for a while. He's like a little puppy, whining and wiggling around its own tail.

"Relax. They didn't fire me." I tell him how Sarah saved the day.

"Rach! You're so mean. I'm glad I didn't come that day. I did it on purpose."

"And you're calling *me* mean?" I want to slap him, I'm so mad. I get up and find another seat at the back of the bus then I remember what Sarah said about harvesting pain. I go back. He looks surprised.

"Why did you do it? Why did you want to hurt me?"

He looks at me as if I'm a dimwit. "Because you broke my heart, Rachel."

"I'm sorry," I say. "I thought we agreed it was best to end things sooner rather than later."

"Frankly, Rach, I thought that was complete bullshit." He has a wild look in his eyes. "I loved you, Rach. I didn't want to lose you. I agreed so that I could be near you in case you changed your mind."

I feel his pain. "Sorry," I apologize again. And then, maybe because I'm so emotional, I blab, "I've been working on this poem, and I want you to know that I'm happy for you. For having a new girlfriend."

"Well, thanks. Nat is cool, but she's not you." His eyes pierce mine, and I realize he wants to get back together. And in the same moment, I know I never really loved him. I just enjoyed the attention and the pretense of being in love.

I shiver. This revelation is so intense, it shakes me to the core. I broke up with him not because love ended, but because it never existed in the first place. The realization is freeing.

Chase sees my reaction. He looks confused, and I'm afraid he's going to say something too direct, which will hurt us both, but on the other hand, I want to run toward the pain. I want to run toward it with my arms spread as if to hug it, to embrace it as part of my being.

Chase's expression changes. While I'm galloping toward the pain, he runs away from it. "Wait, did you say something about writing a poem?" He chuckles. "Rachel Davis, a poem? Really?"

I laugh and cry at the same time. I put my hand on his cheek. "Chase. You and I. It's…" I shake my head. I struggle to find the right words, and then I hear myself say, "I'm in love with this woman, Sarah Walters."

Chase flinches. He looks puzzled as he moves away from me as if I'm some kind of monster. He says something, but I don't hear him.

Oh my god. I put my hands on my burning cheeks. *I'm in love with Sarah.*

 ecca

FINALLY, back at work, I'm still a faded version of who I used to be. I'm minding my own business when the hum of the office turns into a deep hush. There's a disturbance in the regular, mildly energetic vibe.

I shiver when I hear a familiar voice.

"Lia," she's saying. "Lia."

It must be my imagination. But there she is. Her hair is spread over her shoulders like a beautiful fan. She's wearing casual skinny jeans and a plaid shirt, but she's gorgeous no matter what she's in. All eyes are on her, and it's easy because we have glass walls. She's at the receptionist's station, who points her in my direction. My heart misses a beat.

She locks eyes with me and starts walking in my direction. I think I'm going to swoon. Then she passes me, giving a little smile. She steps into Darren's corner office.

What is she doing? Is it some sort of revenge?

Not a minute has passed when my phone buzzes, and I'm summoned to the corner office.

"Becca, this is Lia Green," Darren says. He touches her upper arm. It makes me furious.

Lia gives me a devious smile and reaches out her hand. "Nice to meet you," she says.

I can't speak. I shake her hand. Her palm is warm and strong. She puts her other palm on top of our handshake and caresses my hand with her thumb. My knees are weak.

"Becca Davis is one of our senior CPAs." He presents me, conveniently forgetting to mention that I'm the Head of Finance.

Lia frowns. "I was under the impression I was going to meet an executive."

What is she doing? She knows my position.

"Yes, yes, of course," Darren says in the smooth, ingratiating manner I hate. "Becca is the Head of Finance."

"So why didn't you say so in the first place?" she scorns. "I don't want to work with a firm who discriminates against women." She stands up and straightens her top. She looks very determined, and I love her so much.

"I'm so sorry. I must have given you the wrong impression. Please." Darren points at the chair. "Can I get you something? Coffee? Tea?"

She gives him a condescending look. It's the same look she gives trainees who slack off during a workout.

"Are you going to be the one who makes the coffee, or is it going to be one of your minion women secretaries?"

Darren is speechless. I've never seen him like that before, and I quite enjoy it.

Lia turns to me. Her doe-like brown eyes are smiling. "Well, Mrs. Davis. Or is it a Ms.?"

I grin.

Darren clears his throat. "Well, Becca, Ms. Green here is

going to open a gym. And she needs our help setting up her business plan."

"Really, Lia? That's great!" I beam at her and reach for her hand reflexively.

She lets me hold her hands, and I'm filled with such joy.

"Wait, you two know each other?" Darren is confused.

Lia's look is challenging. *Go on*, her eyes say, *you know what you need to do.*

I take a deep breath. This is my moment to shine. "Lia is my girlfriend." I don't take my eyes off hers. "She's the love of my life," I add.

Darren falls back into his chair. Lia's deep grin is my reward.

I frame her face with my hands. She nods slightly. The entire office stops breathing, and I don't care. She came back to me. She came.

I lean forward to kiss her.

achel

IT TAKES two weeks of hard work before *So You Have a New Girlfriend* turns into a beautiful, shiny piece of literature. Sarah and I dissect it inside out, discussing every word, every comma, and every row break. Then we dissect it at the macro level, making sure that every theme, every emotion, every innuendo is in place. I'm proud of the result. It's so me. Sure, Sarah helped me dig deep into my soul, but the words are mine. They express my beliefs and my thought process.

The emotions portrayed in the piece are those I feel for her, and not what I'd ever felt about Chase, but it doesn't matter because love is love. And I love her. I love my poem too.

It also makes me want to barf. The poem, that is. I've read and reread it so many times that the words haunt me when I'm awake and penetrate my dreams when I sleep. I'm sick of it.

"That's good," Sarah says when I tell her how I feel about the poem. I don't dare tell her what I feel for her.

"That's how you tell when your work is done," she says.

"Really?" I can't believe it. I'm happy we did it, but I'm also sad. Does it mean we're done? *Is it the right time to tell her how I feel about her?*

"We should celebrate. Your first poem." Sarah's eyes sparkle with pride and joy. "Wait here, I'm going to get us some ice cream." She runs out to the street, and I watch her from the window. She comes back minutes later, holding two large sundaes.

We sit quietly for a while, eating our sundaes.

"Rachel Davis, I think it's time. You're ready to spread your wings and fly away."

"No," I whisper. Goosebumps crawl over my spine.

"Trust me, Rachel. You're ready. Now, I did some research. There's a small-scale slam event in Joliet this weekend. It's in the community center, and it's a great place to make your first appearance. No one you know will be there, so you can suck, and it won't have any repercussions."

"Oh. I thought you meant this. Us." I say with relief when I realize she's talking about the poem.

"I've already signed you up." She smiles a mischievous smile and wipes whipped cream off her face.

"What? That's three days away!"

"Yeah." She shrugs. "Wait. You want to stop this mentorship? Why?"

"No. I thought *you* wanted to end it. Because you can't beat the block," I whisper.

She waves dismissively.

"So, Friday. I want to spend the night at Tamara's, my sister. You're welcome to join me. There's an extra air mattress. And you'll love Hayden, my niece. She's such a sweetie-pie."

It's nice to hear about her world. Usually, we talk about mine. "I'd like that." My heart races at the thought of spending the night next to Sarah.

"Great. We'll have a slumber party." She smiles and touches my arm.

It's like I've been hit by lightning. Electricity flows from her to me, charging me with a sweet sensation. I don't want her ever to take her hand away.

CHAPTER 8

ecca

"I'VE MISSED YOU SO MUCH," Lia says. We're sitting downstairs at Barrow's. It's the dead time between the end of breakfast service and just before lunch. So it's just the two of us in the entire place. We order coffee because we have to order something, but we don't touch our steaming mugs. We're holding hands, and I'm not letting go. Not even for the best coffee in town.

"I thought I would never see you again," I say.

Her soft brown eyes are full of tears. "I wanted to call you a million times, Bex. I'm so ashamed."

"It doesn't matter anymore. We're back together again, right?" I wipe her tears with my thumbs. Our fingers are still interlaced, and her hand drags with mine like I'm a puppeteer.

She shakes her head, and I panic. *Does she mean we're not back together? Is this just a break in the breakup?*

"I was wrong to demand you come out." Then she laughs. "Although, I'm glad you did what you did back there in the office. It was amazing!"

"Right?" I grin. I can't believe I just kissed her in front of the whole staff.

She's sobbing now, and I can't help but sob with her. "I'm so ashamed, Bexy. It was selfish to pressure you. After everything you've been through with Rachel… It was so stupid to break up because of that. I'm such a fool."

Her nose gets red. She sniffles. A passing waiter puts a box of Kleenex on our table. Now we have to release our grip so we can both wipe our runny noses. That makes us laugh again.

She says, "We were great for four months. You handled everything perfectly. I mean, you were on top of everything. Your teenage daughter and her phases, your top executive work. These things were a constant in your life even before me, and then we met, and you handled that beautifully as well. We were getting along so great." She pauses. "Remember when you said you self-sabotage your relationships?"

I nod, even though I don't remember the context.

"It was me who was sabotaging our relationship all along," Lia says. She pokes herself, and she cries and laughs at the same time. "Well, after I practically asked you to marry me on our first date!"

I chuckle. That's a good memory.

"I think we were going too fast, and that intimidated me," she says and grabs my hands again. She caresses my palms with her thumbs. "And when you came to my class— Poof! It was like…" Her eyes shift to the left. She's trying to find the right words. "I thought you were rubbing it in my face, flirting in front of me with stinky Zach, but you came because you wanted to reconcile, right?"

I nod. "Yes. But I thought you'd moved on. That blonde—"

"Who? Trish?" She waves her hand in dismissal. Our hands are still attached, which means my hand is also waving.

"I came because Rachel is finally over her phase—"

"Oh! Really?" She cuts me off mid-sentence. "Did you tell her about me? What did she say? Wait. I'm doing it again, aren't I? You don't have to tell her about me."

Her enthusiasm is charming. My heart is overwhelmed with love. I smile. "Well, I'll certainly tell her now. Because we're back together, right?" I lean my forehead on hers.

Her face lights up. "I can't believe you kissed me in front of Darren. By the way, he's so full of it. Exactly like you said!"

"I know! Right?" But what I really want to know is, are we back together? Because I've asked her twice already and twice, she's changed the subject.

A waiter stops by our table and clears his throat to get our attention. He hands us the menus, but we're not about to lose our grip for that. We make him feel uncomfortable. He puts the menus on the table. "Ladies, our kitchen is open for orders," he says quickly before he disappears.

People start flowing into the place. Soon it will be packed.

Lia releases my hands and leans back. I shiver. This is the moment of truth.

"Bex, where have you been?" she asks quietly.

"What do you mean?"

She hesitates for a minute. "I've called your office each day for, I don't know, was it two weeks? I had to make sure you were there when I made my appearance because that was the whole point. I'm not going to open a gym, by the way."

"That's too bad. Because you'd rock it."

She shrugs and looks at her phone. It's been vibrating like

crazy for the past few minutes. I get the feeling our time is almost up.

"Did you want to prank me?" I smile. "Is that why you came to the office? Because I got a vibe when I saw you pass me, and frankly, I was horrified."

She chuckles. But only with her mouth. Her eyes remain serious. "You know me so well," she says. "It started out as a revenge plan. For flirting with Zach. But as time passed, and you weren't there, I began questioning my motives, and I realized how foolish I was. And the plan, well, let's just say it morphed into not so much as revenge, but as a way to test the waters. See if you're still interested."

I shake my head. "I've been on sick leave. Since that day at the gym."

"Oh." Her brown eyes are filled with remorse, but then she smiles. "Still can't believe you kissed me in the office. He was so shocked!"

A sudden fear clenches my lungs, and I struggle for air. What will Sheila say? Will she fire me? Will she deny my promotion?

"Bex? Are you okay?" Lia grabs my hands again.

"Lia," I whisper. "Are we back together? Please, I need to know."

"Of course we are, silly. I mean, that's what you want, right?" She frowns.

I nod. "More than anything else," I whisper.

"Then that's settled." She gets up. "Need to run, Bexy. Laters?" She plants a kiss on my cheek.

My hands are shaking. I'm so relieved. I take a sip of the coffee; it's completely cold.

I stay at Barrow's for a while after she leaves. I'm too embarrassed to go back upstairs and face my colleagues. I feel like in those dreams when I come to work naked and everybody is staring. It takes time to gather enough courage to go back upstairs. A text from Lucy does the trick.

Congrats on your new gf. Ppl are thrilled!!!! After about 20 exclamation marks there is an emoji of two girls standing next to each other.

Lucy shrieks with joy when I step out of the elevator two minutes later. She rushes toward me, hugs me, and says she didn't know I was such a Millennial. I don't know what she means, but I thank her politely. It's nice to be accepted.

On the short walk to my office, people go out of their way to express their joy regarding my new status, congratulating me and asking how we met and how long we've been together. I never realized how popular I am, and it's great to see how supportive they are. My fears evaporate.

Well, until I see Darren's frowzy, frowny face.

"Well, Becca, I've wanted to get rid of you for quite a while now, and I finally have a winning hand," he gloats.

"Why? Does it make me a bad CPA just because I date a gorgeous woman? That's discrimination," I protest.

"Tell that to Sheila," he says and walks with me to her office. She looks serious.

The hell with it all. Maybe Lia isn't going to open her own gym, but I can certainly open my own accounting firm. I know for a fact that some of our clients would follow me blindly wherever I go. Sheila pulls the blinds down. The last thing I see is Darren's ghastly smile.

"Becca," Sheila says. She moves toward me and grabs my hands. Then she drops them. Maybe she thinks I'm contagious. But then she says the most amazing and unexpected thing. "Would you and your girlfriend like to join my wife and me for dinner on Friday night?"

I gasp. *Sheila?* Who would have thought? "I have to ask Lia, but sure, I'd love to meet your wife." I step out of her office with my head held high.

Darren is hanging around by the door. He probably expected me to come out crying. I pass him and don't say a word.

As I'm picking my phone to call Lia, I discover a new text from Rachel.

Heads up. Going to spend Friday night at Dad's. Back Saturday morn. Do not freak out!

I know there's no way she's going to spend the night at Jason's. I'm sure crazy, pregnant Renee wouldn't like that. No. It must be Chase. It makes me so happy. What was a great day up until that moment, suddenly turns into the best day ever.

Lia uses her seductive tone when I call to tell her. She says, "Let's meet with Sheila some other time and have a romantic night on Friday. I believe you owe me one."

I can't help but laugh. "Will you stay over? Wake up next to me? Will you help me break the news to Rachel when she returns?"

"Yes, yes, and hell yes!"

I can't see her, but I can feel her grin.

achel

FRIDAY, I'm the clumsiest. I don't know what's freaking me out the most—reading my poem in front of a bunch of strangers or spending the night at Sarah's sister's house. My mood swings dramatically. One minute, I'm extremely happy and can't stop smiling. The next, I need to stop myself from texting Sarah and calling the whole thing off. Meanwhile, books slip through my hands as if they're grains of sand. After the third time it happens, Mrs. Ilman looks at me funny and starts following me around. That makes me even more nervous. My hands shake.

I drop a heavy Norman Rockwell while re-shelving the art section. It hits the floor with a deep thud. Mrs. Ilman erupts. "What's wrong with you today? Are you sick?" She touches my forehead then pulls her hand back quickly as if she's been bitten by a snake.

"You're burning up!" she announces. Everyone who's

nearby, including her, hurries to move away from me to a safer distance.

But I'm not contagious. I'm burning with desire, and the only way to catch it is by falling in love.

I try to keep a low profile and reply with, "Sorry, Mrs. Ilman." She sends me home on sick leave, prescribing lots of fluids and tons of rest for the weekend. Yeah, right. As if. "Yes, Mrs. Ilman," I say humbly.

Sarah calls when I'm on the bus heading home.

"I've convinced my roommate to lend me her car. Are you up for a drive?"

We were planning to get the Amtrak Lincoln service. A car is much better.

"Sure!"

"Pick you up at your place?"

My heart pounds at the thought of Sarah coming to my house.

"Oh, and I've just checked the forecast. Heavy showers are expected later in the afternoon," she says. "So I'd like to leave as early as possible.

I look at the clock on my phone. "Hmmm... how about noon-ish?" That would give me about an hour to get ready.

Mom's at work and I invade her closet, looking for the perfect outfit for my performance. I don't know why I do it; I've never done it before. We're not even the same dress size. She prefers smart-casual while I'm more of a streetwear kind of girl. Although hoodies and leggings are quite acceptable at Spoken Word events, I feel they don't fit my poem, which requires a more sophisticated look.

I DON'T HAVE a lot of time to go through all her clothes, so I just pick up the first thing that catches my eye, a floral dress. When I try it on, it looks exactly like what it is—a little girl wearing her mama's clothes. No time to waste, my second choice need to be right. I find a stretchy black dress I've never seen Mom wear. It hugs my body snugly; I look so womanly. Perfect. I find a pair of knee-high black boots with stiletto heels. I wonder why she owns these—she's tall enough as it is. They look slutty, which isn't even remotely close to her style. Lucky for me though, we wear the same shoe size.

I pull my hair up and put on some eyeliner and lipstick then step back to examine the new me. Wow. It takes me a minute to recognize myself. The new outfit makes me look older. Smarter. But it lacks color. A scarf, perhaps? I open Mom's scarf drawer and flinch.

I did not expect to find a lacy corset there. Something resembling a dildo peeks from underneath. It's too much of a shock. I close the drawer with a bang, wishing I could unsee it.

Then it hits me. *Mom has a lover.* A slow grin spreads across my face. I wonder who it might be. She must have met him at the gym. That would explain why she'd been hanging out there so much lately. I have another *aha* moment. They must have had a lover's quarrel. *That's* why she stopped going.

But why didn't she tell me about him? Is he way younger than her? Can it be that Mom's a cougar? I dismiss this thought with laughter. Mom's too conservative. He must have other flaws. Maybe he's married. Or poor. Or he doesn't have a college degree. Yeah, that's probably it. She can't tell me about her uneducated lover while pressuring me to go to college.

Then I freeze in place. *Could it be the other way around? She doesn't want to introduce me? The young, disturbed daughter?* All these thoughts drive me crazy, and I can't deal with it right now. I already have enough crazy of my own. Sarah will be here in a few minutes, and I still have to pack my overnight bag.

Suddenly, I'm charged with erotic energy. I think about Mom's corset. *I wish I could pull off wearing something like that.* The thought of Sarah seeing me wearing lingerie makes me all warm and shivery. I remember what she said at our first meeting, about never turning anyone who didn't want to be turned. *Oh god, please turn me.*

Then I realize how stupid it is to use the word 'turn.' Love is love. When you love somebody, you're blind about their gender. *Tonight, after the event, I'm going to tell her how I feel about her.*

There's so much at stake tonight, probably the rest of my life, but I find myself mulling over my kitten pajamas. Should I pack them or not? On the one hand, I love their fuzzy comfort; on the other, they're quite childish. What would Sarah think?

The doorbell rings and cuts short my contemplation. It's Sarah. *Can she tell I was thinking about her?*

She looks tired and kind of ragged without her makeup. Her bangs shine with green stripes; the rest of her crest is hidden under a gray slouchy hat. She's wearing a green sweater, skinny jeans, and heavy boots. I'm clearly over-dressed. My armpits begin to moisten even though there's a freezing wind blowing outside.

"Wow, Rach! Look at you!"

"Too much, huh? I didn't think it through. Sorry. I'll change."

"No, wait," she calls after me. "You look great! Don't change."

I flush. Now I'm even more embarrassed. "Would you like to come in? I'm not done packing yet." My voice is so high-pitched, I'm basically chirping.

"How long will you be?" She lights up a cigarette.

"I thought you quit."

She frowns. "I'll wait in the car." She points toward a faded blue Corolla parked on the other side of the street. Her hand shakes.

Why does she look so nervous? What's going on?

ecca

THIS WEEK HAS BEEN an emotional roller coaster. The word about me having a girlfriend spread like wildfire. One of our loyal clients, Milford & Sons, announced they'll be looking for a different accounting firm. Well, at first they negotiated better terms, which included me not working there anymore. I'm sure it was relentless Darren who encourged them to fire me, although I can't prove it. Luckily, Sheila cut that in the bud. Come Friday, I'm so stressed and emotionally drained. I'm anticipating the romantic evening with Lia, yet memories of our last attempt to have a night at my house keep haunting me. I've got my second chance with her; there won't be another one. So much hangs on this one evening, I'm terrified.

I take a personal day, but I get ready for work as I usually do to avoid any prying questions.

Rachel and I eat our breakfast quietly. We each have thoughts that torment us, knowing that tonight is going to be an important night for the both of us. She still hasn't told me any details about her plans. Does she think I swallowed her lame tale about spending the night at Jason's?

Her cheeks are rosy, her hair falling over her eyes as she concentrates on her cereal bowl. I watch, eating hurriedly, avoiding eye contact, and I'm filled with tender, motherly love. My heart goes out to her as I lean over and tuck a bunch of hair behind her ear. She looks up, puzzled.

"Mom!" Her tone is resentful.

"Sorry." But I can't stop myself. "I know this seems out of the blue, but how are you in regard to protection?"

"Huh?"

"You know...*protection*..."

Her cheeks turn red. "Mom, I'm not a child."

"Yeah, yeah." I raise my hands in surrender, "I don't want to interfere in your life, I just want to make sure you're not doing anything foolish."

"Right back at you," she says calmly and goes back to eating her breakfast.

Now I'm freaking out. "What do you mean?"

"Well, *you* didn't use protection when you were my age, right? That's how I came into this world," she says calmly.

This conversation backfired quickly. Now it's my turn to turn red because she gets straight to the point. I'm babbling. "It wasn't like that...we wanted to have you—"

"Yeah, yeah." She cuts me off mid-apology. "I've heard it all before. But you can rest assured—I'm not going to get pregnant anytime soon. Happy now?" And with these parting words, she gets up and puts her bowl and spoon in the dishwasher.

A few minutes later she's gone to work, and I'm still sitting at the kitchen table. I need something relaxing; I need a class with Lia.

The receptionist at the gym says Lia's taken a personal day. That's not like her.

Baby, are we still on for 2night? I text.

Hell, yeah! She replies with a smiling emoji that has hearts for eyes.

I move my thumb over the screen as if I'm caressing her pretty face. With a sigh, I get up and start planning my morning in my head. Mani-pedi, a stop by the hair stylist, and then the market to get produce for a romantic dinner for two.

Around noon I get back, my hands full of groceries. There's a distinctive smell; I sniff the air. It smells like someone was smoking nearby, and there's a cigarette butt lying on the curb. That's unexpected in this neighborhood, and it makes me feel funny, a bit anxious. As I reach for my key, I notice the front door is slightly ajar. Fear crawls up my spine. *We've been robbed.*

A noise comes from inside the house, and I realize the robbers are still inside. Now my fear turns into panic. *What do I do?* My hands are full with groceries; I can't reach for my purse to get my phone. There's no one in the street to help me. I stand still by the door and calculate my options.

Then it swings open, and there's Rachel. Both of us scream at the same time.

"Mom! What are you doing here?"

"Why is the door open? I thought it was a burglar!"

"Oops, that's just—"

"What are you wearing? Are those my boots?"

A rosy blush flourishes in Rachel's cheeks, and she quickly moves away, skipping down the stairs.

"I've borrowed some clothes," she yells over her shoulder. "Bye, Mom. See you tomorrow!" She rushes toward a dinged-up car parked on the other side of the street.

"Is that Chase?" I call, but she just waves her hand. I put down the groceries bags and run after her. I can't tell who's driving. He's wearing a hat, and his face is turned the other way.

Rachel gets in the passenger seat, and as the driver speeds away, the window rolls down, and a cigarette butt is thrown out. I catch a glimpse of his face in the side mirror, and all I can see are piercing green eyes, and I know for a fact that it's not Chase.

With pure panic, I try to call Rachel. She doesn't pick up. The Corolla speeds up and disappears around the curve. I call again. She still doesn't pick up, but she texts me.

Stop calling me!!!! I'm fine. See you tomorrow

I text back, *Where are you going? Who's with you?* Radio silence.

I stand in the street for about two minutes before I give up. She's not going to reply.

I'm so angry, I feel my blood boiling in my veins as I pick up my groceries and go inside. I want to slap her. How dare she treat me like that? There's a note on the fridge

Mom, borrowed a black dress and boots. Heart R.

The heart mellows some of my frustration. I crumble the note and throw it into the recycling bin. My fingers tap the phone keys; it's an uncontrollable impulse.

"What?" Jason barks into the phone. I guess it's because he's near *her.* But I have no intention of playing his little game.

I hang up.

He calls a second later. "Sorry for that." He sounds too apologetic. "I thought you were someone else."

"Who, Renee?"

He doesn't reply. Any other time I would get some weird satisfaction from delving into it, but not right now. I'm too pissed. I know what he's going to say, but I still need to ask. "Are you meeting Rachel today?"

"No." He's alert. He still knows me too well. "What's going on, B? Is everything okay?"

I sigh. What do I tell him? I want to vent, but it's such a delicate matter. As angry as I am with our daughter, I don't want to betray her trust. "Probably nothing." I chuckle. "Rachel took my boots."

"What boots?"

"She just took off with a funny-looking dude."

"Funny how?"

"He looked... I don't know." I try to recall the glimpse I'd gotten of those piercing eyes. "Old. He looked wrinkly around the eyes."

Jason sighs. "I want to make sure I've got this straight. Are you accusing me because Rachel's dating an older guy?"

"Yeah. No. What?" I'm confused. *How did he get there?*

"It's not like Renee was a gold-digger looking for a dying man. We're only twelve years apart, and it's not like I'm loaded."

"Jason. Stop. I wasn't implying that it was your fault and if you thought that, I apologize. I just wanted to share my concern."

"Oh, okay. Sorry for heating up," he says after a few seconds.

There's an awkward silence, and I'm about to hang up when I hear myself say, "Jace, can I tell you something?"

"Yeah."

"Promise you won't freak out?"

"I'm already freaked out, B. What's going on?"

I take a deep breath. "It's— I'm dating someone."

"You don't need my permission. You know that, right?"

"Jace."

"What? Becca. Say it already!" His tone is vexed.

"It's a woman. I'm dating a woman."

There's a moment of silence as his breath shortens. There're distinct noises of dishes clanking and people talking in the background. He's probably on his lunch.

"Say something."

"Hang on." The noises fade. I'm guessing he's stepped outside.

"Have you always been into women?" he finally asks in a whisper.

"I don't know. Never really thought about it. I'm into *a* woman. Her name is Lia. She's a personal trainer."

He pauses for a few seconds. I can hear the wind whistling. It's blowing wildly.

"I need some time to adjust, I guess. How did Rachel take it?"

I hesitate for a minute. "Haven't told her yet. Please don't say anything if she talks to you."

"Fine," he says.

We're both quiet for a minute. I'm anxious and relieved at the same time.

"B," he finally says. His voice is soft. "Are you happy?"

"Very happy," I say without thought. And I realize it's true. I am happy. *So* happy. I don't care about Rachel's recklessness, or about the fact that she took the boots I was going to wear for my romantic night. That's all nothing but superficial details.

He sighs. "That's good. You deserve to be happy."

I smile. Of course, he can't see it. But he feels it. I can feel him smiling as well.

"I'd like to meet her. Someday. When you're ready," he says.

achel

SARAH IS A TERRIBLE DRIVER. I notice it the moment she speeds out of the parking space and the wheels screech. I fasten my seatbelt and hold on to the door handle. The car is filthy. There's dust on the dashboard, and lots of trash piled on the floor. An empty bottle rolls over my foot and startles me when Sarah hits the curve too quickly.

"Sorry about that," Sarah says. "I didn't know it was in such a state."

For a second, I think she means her driving.

"Is that your mom?" she asks when I reject the phone calls.

"Yep. Did you see her?"

"Just a glimpse. She looks young, though. I thought— Well, with all the pressure about college, I imagined she would be way older."

"She's 38."

"Huh. Only eight years older than me. Weird."

I shift uncomfortably in my seat, and not just because of the way she drives. I didn't think about our age difference, and now I'm freaking out a little, thinking this might be an issue. *What if she thinks I'm too young for her?* It's cold in the car; I rub my hands together.

"Yeah, sorry about that. Heat is broken too."

We should have stuck with our original plan and taken the train. I don't say it out loud.

"Guess we should have taken the Lincoln service, huh? This isn't much of an improvement," Sarah says.

"No, it's fine."

She gives me a quick glance. "Come on, be honest. It's a shitty car, and I'm a lousy driver."

I chuckle. "To be honest, you *are* a lousy driver. And honestly, yes, I think we *would* have been better off taking the Lincoln service."

She frowns. "You're right. What was I thinking?" She shakes her head. "I know I'm a terrible driver, I just thought … well, I wanted to have some privacy."

"Well, since I want to get there alive, how about I drive instead?"

She smiles and pulls over. Still, there's an awkward silence when I take the wheel.

"So did you have an argument with your mother? From the brief moment I caught her eyes she looked annoyed," Sarah asks.

"Forget about it."

"Isn't she supportive? She looks like the kind of mom who'd go to Joliet to cheer for her daughter at her first dip in the Spoken world."

"Yeah, she'd probably do that if she knew. Told her I'm spending the night at my dad's. Guess that cover was just blown."

"Why?"

I shrug. The temperature drops significantly, and the showers start. The wipers aren't functioning very well, and they just smear the water from side to side. With the fog settling in, I can barely see the road. I drive slowly, maybe too slow for even the slow lane. The radio is stuck on one channel, broadcasting what seems to be political banter.

So far, this road trip has been a nightmare. I'm about to give up, just turn back and call it a day when Sarah asks, "Are you ashamed of me? Is that why you didn't tell your mother about me?"

"What? No! I'm ashamed of— It's just my mother is so conservative. She wouldn't understand why I write. Why I need to do this. She'd just yell at me to stop wasting my life. And I don't need that kind of support, thank you."

"Finish the sentence." She orders, "I'm ashamed of..."

I hesitate for a minute. "Me." I flush and wish I could hide from Sarah's intense look.

She laughs that vulgar laugh that I've learned to love. It gives me goosebumps. She puts her hand on my thigh. I get it. She wants to comfort me. It's nice. My blood is hotter there, under her touch.

"Better now?" she asks, and I nod. She leaves her hand on my thigh until we reach Tamara's.

Tamara's apartment is small and crowded, full of furniture and children's toys. Hayden is wearing a pink princess dress and working on a princess jigsaw puzzle when we enter. She's so delighted that she leaves everything and hops over, calling, "Auntie Sawah." We all laugh from the cuteness dust she spreads around.

Sarah lifts her up and spins her around while the little girl shrieks with joy. "Would you like to say hello to Rachel?" Sarah asks. She's a bit short of breath from all the spinning.

Hayden rests her little head on Sarah's shoulder. From

her safe place, she examines me. She has Sarah's eyes. I can see her trying to figure me out, to decide whether she likes me or not. I'm probably more timid than she is. I don't know how to treat children. I stand there, feeling stupid, waving and saying hello with my squeaky voice. Hayden looks into her auntie's eyes and laughs. Is she making fun of me? I can't tell. I wish I knew what to do with my arms and legs. I just sway from side to side; those stilettos were not a good idea.

Sarah breaks the awkwardness. "I have a present for you," she singsongs.

Hayden cries with joy and claps her hands.

"But first, you must say hello to Rachel."

The little girl looks at me again; her head is back in the safe place on Sarah's shoulder. I smile at her, and she smiles back and whispers, "Hello."

"Hello," I whisper too.

"Do you have a present for me?" she whispers, and I shake my head. "Sorry. No."

Her pretty little face crumples up, and her eyes fill with tears. It takes a few minutes and candy to make her stop crying.

I feel so out of place as I apologize to Tamara for not bringing anything for her daughter.

"It's actually great you didn't bring a present. She's so spoiled. She thinks that whenever someone walks through that door, they owe her a shiny object. And she has so much already." Tamara is trying to smooth things over, gesturing to all the toys lying around. It's nice of her but I'm still embarrassed.

While Sarah goes wild with Hayden, playing catch and running in circles, I sit on the couch and try to look cool. I'm not dressed to be running about. Tamara sits by me and tries to make conversation, which doesn't go very well. As much as I try, I can't compose a coherent sentence or even a word with more than one syllable. Lucky for me, Hayden cries a lot, interrupting the conversation as Tamara rushes to sooth her.

We sit down to have some snacks. Hayden gets to choose what we're all going to eat, and she picks grilled cheese sandwiches. Tamara makes them, and Sarah sets the table with Hayden. I'm still sitting on the couch, playing with my phone. I don't belong here.

After we eat, I offer to help Tamara clean up the kitchen, and she accepts my offer with a smile. She gives me an apron so I won't stain my pretty dress. Meanwhile, Sarah tries to put Hayden down for her nap. It doesn't seem to be working; we keep hearing giggles over the baby monitor.

"You and Sarah are perfect for each other," Tamara says. I gasp. I try to explain we're not together, but then Hayden cries again, and Tamara puts down the washcloth and rushes to the nursery. She comes back with Hayden in her hands. Sarah follows them, frowning, trying to say it's not her fault.

Tamara sits Hayden on the counter.

"Mommy, my tummy feels funny," Hayden says, then leans over and throws up all over me. The dress is ruined; the boots are dripping sick.

"Oh, I'm so sorry," Tamara says. She kneels down and starts wiping the boots. "Give me your dress, I'll wash it for you. Or better yet, I'll buy you a new dress. Oh god, this is so embarrassing."

I don't have anything else to wear but my kitten jammies. I'm so miserable. The night is ruined.

Sarah laughs when she sees me.

"You'll certainly be the talk of the day at Spoken," she says as she hugs me in an attempt to comfort me.

Tamara opens her closet for me. She's shorter and skinnier than me, so nothing fits. But then she hands me some of her husband's clothes, which are huge, but at least I can zip them up.

"Wow," Tamara says when I emerge from the bedroom wearing one of Philip's suits.

Sarah concurs. "It suits you," she says and laughs at her pun. The feminine boots, all cleaned up now, add a nice twist to my outfit. It feels like a Halloween costume, as if I dressed up as a drag queen, but funnily it makes me feel secure, like, this is my disguise, my mask. It permits me to be someone else.

Sarah changes before we leave. *I should have done that too.* Worn something casual for the drive and changed before the event. Well, it's too late now.

Sarah's wearing a glittery green dress and silver pumps. The green shades in her hair complement her complexion and deepen her eyes. She's gorgeous.

"Shall we?" she asks and slides her hand in mine as we walk outside. The street is white. Apparently, the showers have turned into snow.

ecca

I SLAVE all afternoon for Lia, thinking her smile will make it all worthwhile. There's celery soup for the appetizer and shrimp pasta with creamy tomato-basil sauce for the entree. There's also a dessert. Her favorite.

I listen to Sia while cooking. Her vocals sooth my nerves. The cooking also helps. Everything is simmering on the stove when I get a phone call from Sheila.

"Becca, I know you're on a personal day, but do you mind swinging by the office for a few minutes?" She sounds cheerful, but knowing her, that doesn't necessarily mean good news.

That's a few minutes at the office plus forty minutes' drive back and forth. I won't have time to get ready or even be back home before Lia arrives.

Anxiously, I just put on my shoes and don't bother dressing up or even fixing my hair. I'm guessing that after the big reveal on Tuesday, no one will even care. *Be there in twenty,* I text Sheila when I'm on my way. *She's not going to fire me, is she?* That could have waited until Monday. *What's the crisis? Did we lose another client?*

I intend to go straight to her office, but I see the whole firm crowding together in the conference room, and I stop to see what's going on. I peek inside and see Ronnie, the silent named partner, seated next to Sheila. He looks tense.

What's going on?

A woman who I don't recognize is sitting next to Sheila. She scans the room intrudingly. Her eyes look smart. *Who is she?*

People are speculating about the purpose of this urgent meeting. Are we in trouble? Is the firm going bankrupt?

"Good, you're here," Sheila says when she notices me. People turn to look at me. I wonder if she picked this specific moment to announce her retirement. According to plan, she's supposed to announce it in August.

Ronnie is slumping in his seat. He doesn't say anything, but I can see all over his face that he's not happy with what's going on.

Sheila clears her throat. Everyone turns quiet. She looks around the room, making brief eye contact with every one of the staff. A small smile spreads across her face.

Oh, no. Terrible scenarios flash through my mind. *She's going to say she's dying. She's terminally ill.* Tears fill my eyes, and I gasp. She's played such a huge part in my life, always encouraging and supporting me. Then it hits me. *I'm writing her eulogy.* The thought makes me so sad.

"A few days ago, our own Becca took a brave step and exposed her sexual preferences in front of all of us. With her brave action, she forced us all to look deep inside ourselves and confront our own beliefs and prejudices. Her public statement caused quite the turmoil in the office, as you all know, with Milford & Sons, one of Becca's biggest and most devoted clients, leaving us after their demand to fire Becca was declined."

There's rustling around the room, and Sheila lifts her hand. The whispers turn into shushes.

"Don't worry. We shall prevail. I've gathered you all here to announce a change in office policy, which falls in line with my beliefs. As of today, we're declaring ourselves an LGBT-owned firm, and with that note, I would like to introduce you all to my wife."

Everyone is overwhelmed when the woman sitting next

to Sheila stands up and nods. She looks to be her late fifties, like Sheila.

"This is Sasha. She's a freelance journalist."

The crowd shifts. People push through to reach Sheila. Everyone wants to congratulate her or introduce themselves to Sasha. Everyone but Darren, who squeezes through them toward the door. He looks yellow, and there's a good reason. His purge attempt has failed. I'm so blessed to have a boss like Sheila.

I'd love to stay and chat, but I can't. When I catch Sheila's eyes, I wave and gesture that I must leave. She nods in agreement and waves me off.

I'm so overwhelmed by what's just happened that I keep taking my attention off the road. Drivers beep like crazy. *Okay, okay. Focus on the road.* But I keep seeing Sheila, standing in the conference room, so proud and calm, introducing us to her wife. It's so incredible.

My phone rings when I'm only a minute from home. It's Lia.

"Where are you?" She's angry. "I've been knocking for a good two minutes."

"Oh, Lia. You won't believe what just happened at work!"

"Didn't you say you were taking a day off?" she asks.

"I did. Which reminds me, why are *you* on a day off?"

"Surprise!" she yells, and I can hear her yelling a split second before I hear her on the phone. She's standing by the front door. There are bags by her feet.

"What's that?" I ask casually, and she grins.

"Surprise!" she yells again. She instructs me to takes the bags to the kitchen, where she unpacks several Tupperware boxes full of food. "Tada!" she says proudly. "I took a day off to cook for you."

I laugh hysterically.

She doesn't expect my response; she frowns. "Thought you'd be happy."

"I am," I say when I finally catch my breath. I guide her to the stove. "Only, I did the same thing."

She hugs me. Her head is on my chest, on my breasts, and I lean down to kiss her hair. She shifts her face toward me, and our lips meet. Hers are so soft and welcoming, I feel like I'm sinking; my whole body collapses into this one point. When I open my eyes, I see her watching me with so much love and tenderness.

"I love you," I whisper. "I love you so much."

I carry her two steps, to the counter, where she seats herself. Her legs are still wrapped around my waist and her arms around my neck. She pulls me down to her wanting lips. And there it is, the chemical reaction which fuses us together.

She slides her hands forward, underneath my shirt, and cups my breasts over my bra. My nipples react to her touch, hardening in an instant, and my knees wobble. I breathe heavily. My hands are in her hair, pulling her even closer. I could stay like this forever; I'm so addicted to her touch.

But then she taps on my shoulder and detaches her lips. I lean forward, my eyes still closed, trying to track her mouth.

"Bexy," she whispers. "Let's eat. Please. I'm starving."

I open my eyes. She's so beautiful, with her lips slightly parted and that mesmerizing gap between her upper teeth. I still haven't caught my breath, so I just nod in agreement, and she jumps off the counter and makes herself busy scouting for cutlery and plates in the cabinets. We set the table together for our romantic dinner for two. I light the scented candles I purchased earlier today while she presses oranges for fresh juice.

Casually, while we both work around the kitchen, I tell her what went down in the office. The story excites her, and she stops pressing the citrus and stares at me with her eyes wide. Then she rushes over and hugs me. "Bex! That's great! You've created a chain reaction by coming out in the office. Don't you see that? It's amazing. You probably changed so many lives without even knowing."

I'm embarrassed. I don't deserve this compliment. After all, it just happened. It wasn't intentional. "Oh, and I told my ex about us."

Now she can't contain her enthusiasm. She shrieks with joy and holds her fists to her mouth. "You're full of surprises today!" she says happily.

I smile, remembering that I have a few more surprises up my sleeve. She'd find out about them later tonight.

"What did he say?" She's curious.

"He was quite supportive actually, which was surprising. I thought he would freak out and conspire against me with Rachel."

"Why would he do that?"

I shrug. "I don't know. It was probably just in my head."

Her eyes are sparkling. "So, now there's just Rachel."

"Well," I say, frowning. "Rachel's been through my closet. She took the black boots you got me, can you believe that?"

"So she's definitely *not* going to spend the night at her dad's."

I tell her about the funny-looking dude in the car. She shakes her head and clicks her tongue.

Then I go to the master bedroom and come back with the present I got her. Well, actually, I got it for the both of us. "I hope she didn't find this!" I wave the double-sided dildo.

Lia tilts her head back and laughs her heart out.

While we were chatting, we'd finished setting the table. It looks beautiful with the candles and flowers. Lia pulls out a chair.

"Actually, baby." I stop her mid-sit. "I was planning for

this night to start differently. Do you mind stepping outside for two minutes?"

She shakes her head and chuckles, but she does as I ask.

There's a knock on my front door.

"Just a minute!" I say as I rush to open the door. I'm wearing the corset set with my bunny slippers because it's freezing. Hilarious.

Lia laughs. "Do I have déjà vu?" she asks.

"God. I hope not," I chuckle.

"Love the cute twist you've made to the outfit," she says, laughing again.

I can barely eat a thing, but I take great pleasure in watching her devour the food I've cooked for her. When it's time for dessert, I bring out a rich cinnamon cake shaped like a huge Cinnabon. She claps her hands and screams with delight, like a little girl who's found the present she wanted under the Christmas tree. She reminds me of Rachel, and concern pinches me. I hope she's doing fine, wherever she is. I look out the window. Snow has begun to fall.

"What is it, baby?" Lia places her hand on my exposed leg. Her touch lights me up.

I shake the thoughts about Rachel out of my head. There's nothing I can do. "Would you like to take a bath?" I ask.

"Well," she says, her eyes sparkling. "I'd like to get dirty first.

She draws me close to her and kisses the bare strip of skin between the corset and my panties. She reaches with her tongue underneath the snug fabric and licks my belly button. It's like I'm being electrocuted and tickled at the same time. I giggle uncontrollably.

She reaches for the string that holds the corset in place. I've tied it loosely this time, and she opens it with one pull, whooping as the corset reveals my breasts.

I can see the passion in her eyes as she moves her hands

over my body. My thighs shiver from desire when she slides her hand down into my thong and caresses me gently over the center of my desire.

I can barely stand, so I lean on her while her fingers dance over my folds. Shivers of pleasure go up and down my spine and flow like blood to the tip of my toes. I hold on to her shoulders while my body convulses with the waves of my orgasm.

 achel

THE COMMUNITY CENTER where the Spoken Word event is taking place is warm and nice. Soft music plays in the background, and there are some light refreshments. Only about a dozen people sit in the crowd, those few who were crazy enough to leave their homes in this weather, which is the talk on everybody's lips. *Snow in April*, they say in wonder. *That's global warming for you.*

We mingle. I talk to an old bearded guy wearing a plaid shirt and suspenders. He thinks I'm Sarah's girlfriend. "You've got a good one there," he says as he shifts his weight from heels to toes while hanging onto his suspenders.

I wish. I respond with a smile.

"She's so talented," he says. "I adore the way she makes words dance to her whim."

I nod with agreement. Then a woman approaches. She

looks to be in her mid-twenties, but it's hard to tell because she has so many tattoos and piercings.

"I admire your clothing selection," she says. Her blackened lips move to reveal the braces on her teeth.

"Thanks." I shrug and wonder if I should tell the story behind it.

"It's so nice to see Sarah's settling down," she says, and before I have a chance to correct her, Sarah's next to me. She pulls me aside. Her face is pale, and she looks worried.

"Tamara just called. Hayden is in the hospital. She kept throwing up after we left, and she has a fever, too. One hundred and five, Tamara said. The doctors say she'll be fine but they do want her to stay the night. I don't think we can spend the night." Her eyes look terrified. I grab her hand and try to seem confident.

"I'm sure she'll be fine. She looks like a healthy toddler." She nods absentmindedly, but I can see she's still worried.

And then it's my turn to speak. The presenter calls my name. "Rachel Davis is a new, aspiring poet. She will read a poem titled, *So You Have a New Girlfriend*."

My palms are wet. My pulse is racing. My ears are ringing. There are some faint claps from the crowd. As I go onstage, I hear whispers. People are saying, *this is Sarah's girlfriend*.

Everything is suddenly moving in slow motion. The walk to the stage takes forever, and I need to pee. *What's that expression? Butterflies in the stomach?* It's like I swallowed a whole swarm of them.

And then, I reach the stage and climb up. I face the crowd and see a lot of expectant faces. They seem open and encouraging. They don't want me to fail. They are waiting to be enlightened. Inspired. I look at Sarah's glowing eyes. She sits in the front row, right underneath me.

She nods and gives me a thumbs up. And as I look into

her eyes, I realize this is all wrong. I shouldn't be reading this poem.

I clear my throat. "Forgive me for the mix-up," I say into the microphone. The voice sounds similar to mine, but also different. It's higher and creakier, and I realize it's much worse than I'd always thought. I have a sudden urge to run away. I look for mocking signs on people faces. Those two who are smiling at each other, is it because of my voice?

My eyes lock on Sarah's confident gaze. She nods in reassurance. I inhale deeply. I can't let her down.

My hand shakes as I reach into the suit pocket and pull out a small piece of paper, folded so many times it's already ripped around the seams. "This is called *Rachel*," I say. My voice echoes back. *Ignore it. Just ignore it.* I inhale deeply and close my eyes for a second. "It's a little bit raw. But I hope you like it." I clear my throat.

Sarah rests her chin on her palm. She looks surprised. But she's listening.

A demon sits on my shoulder.
He has my eyes.
Do it, he hisses with his snake-like tongue.
I don't want to die.
Pools of blood.
No, I don't want to die.
I just want to feel.
In my reflection, there's pureness, and there's truth.
In my eyes, there's a sliver of life.

They expect more. I've only used about two minutes of my ten-minute slot, but that's all there is. After a long pause, I say, "Thank you," and get off the stage. I don't hear a thing. I don't see a thing.

Except for Sarah's eyes. They shine toward me when she gets up to greet me. They're the lighthouse guiding me home.

"That was—" she says before she chokes. She moves close

to hug me. Without even thinking about it, I move my face so I can capture her lips. And then, we kiss.

Her lips are creamy and soft. She tastes like mint and ash, and it stings, but in a good way. What starts as a soft kiss quickly ignites, full of desire. Her hands shoot to my face, holding me closer, and I glide mine over her neck. Our kiss deepens as her tongue enters my mouth, searching for my tongue. I open my mouth wider to welcome her, and she consumes me.

When we finally stop for air, I hear the roar. It's the crowd. They're cheering for us.

ecca

WE'RE RELAXING in a bubble bath. It's something I've wanted to do ever since we started dating. Lia's apartment has only a small shower, so this is a special treat. Tea candles set the mood, and we share one glass of red wine, sipping in turns. Well, until Lia kisses me with a mouthful, spilling the wine directly into my mouth. It's like a mama bird feeding her young, and it's so funny.

Everything is quiet around us. The snow falls on the skylight above, and for a while, we just sit quietly. I'm leaning against the tub, and Lia's leaning against me as I caress her arms with my fingers, moving them up and down ever so lightly. Her skin is smooth and silky.

Lia tells me about her day. I listen to her bitching about the gym owners, who are still giving her the shitty shifts, and how she's going to treat the trainers differently in her own gym, which she's totally planning to open because I've inspired her with my bravery. I tell her about a walk-in client who came in the other day and expected me to draft a plan to launder his poker wins.

I could do this every day. Unwind next to her after a long day at work.

When the water gets cold, we slowly rise. We dry each other with thick, fluffy towels and we kiss. All my passion is in that kiss. My tongue swirls around hers, and I hold her close.

She gives in. Her eyes are closed and her mouth half-open as I shower little kisses all over her face. I nibble her lower lip and kiss the edge of her mouth. She moans.

I hold her hand and pull her into the bedroom. We've

never done it in my bed before. It was always at her place, and always kind of quick because I needed to get home early enough not to raise Rachel's suspicions.

Now, we have all the time in the world.

Lia lies on her back and lets me explore her body. Her head tilts back as I glide my lips over her collarbone and my hands cup her little breasts. Her nipples are as hard as her abs. I graze my teeth over them. I don't bite hard, just enough to turn her on.

Her hands are in my hair, massaging my skull as I kiss my way down to her mound. Her musky scent drives me crazy with passion and I need to hold back as I probe her folds gently with just the tip of my tongue. She spreads her legs for me, and I go deeper, stronger. She shivers when I touch her clit. It's so satisfying to feel her reaction. I stroke her labia with my tongue before returning to that little button of pleasure. She trembles under my touch, and I'm so happy I can give her this kind of sensation. When I feel she's close, I press my tongue to her tender spot and stimulate her until she twitches and wiggles and shouts my name.

Smiling, I wait for her to come back. She fondles my cheek, "Bexy," she says. Her voice is angelic and her eyes are so soft. But then she rolls over and shrieks with joy as she tries to put on our new sex toy, a special harness with a double-sided strap-on. I lie on my back with my hands behind my neck, expecting us to fuck each other simultaneously.

But then, I hear someone at the door. We both freeze in place, and I can see my panic reflected in her eyes.

achel

THE DRIVE back from Joliet takes three hours. The roads are icy, so I drive slowly, carefully. One of my hands is on the wheel, and the other is holding Sarah's. Our freezing fingers are interlaced. My cheeks hurt because I can't stop smiling.

Sarah directs me to Home-Cut Donuts by the I-80, where we stop for coffee and double-chocolate donuts. It's nice and warm inside, and we find a nice little niche by the corner which is slightly hidden from the room. We cram next to each other; her body radiates heat. We sit for a while, eating our sweet treats. We laugh and kiss. Small kisses of bliss. Our lips are sticky, but we don't mind.

"That poem of yours," Sarah says. Her lips are close to mine. Her eyes are two drops of a crystal pond.

"I wrote it when I was cutting." I talk slowly.

She watches my lips as they move, nodding with every

word I say. "It's very raw, of course, but it was very moving," she whispers then catches my lower lip with her teeth. "I'm so glad you decided to share it. Maybe the crowd didn't understand, but I, for one, identify."

"You do?"

She leans over and wipes a bit of cream off my chin with her thumb, then she licks it slowly. "It's very you," she says and closes her hand into a fist. "It really captures your essence."

My eyes fill with tears. Her words so move me, I can barely speak.

"That's what I think." My voice is choked. She gets me; she really does understand.

When we finally step out to the car, her arm is around my waist, and mine lies casually over her shoulder, although there's nothing casual about it. I'm so excited to feel her touch and overwhelmed she kissed me back.

It's so cold, we need to stop literally every ten minutes to thaw and warm up. And at each stop, our mouths collide in desperate longing as if it wasn't just minutes since we last kissed.

Sarah is a great kisser. She makes my stomach ache with desire. I've only kissed Chase, so I'm not that experienced. I let her lead. After all, she's my mentor. When she opens her mouth, I open mine. When she tilts her head, I tilt mine. She laughs and tilts it in the opposite direction. I get the hang of it pretty quick. After a few stops, I start to emit low sounds when she put her lips on mine. It feels like all my nerves have been exposed—all it takes is a slight stimulus, and I'm making these feral sounds.

I've never been like this before. Sarah has awakened some wild thing inside me, a part I didn't know even existed. Just feeling her warm breath on my neck makes me want to roar.

"Oh Rachel, you drive me crazy," she whispers in my ear before diving for my lips again.

Pretty soon, kisses are not enough. Her hands slide under my coat, under the suit, under the buttoned-down men's shirt I'm wearing. Her freezing-cold fingers leave hot burn marks everywhere they touch.

When we stop at McDonald's for nuggets and fries, I can barely swallow. My lips are swollen. My stomach is one huge knot of desire.

It's way after midnight when I pull up in front of my house. Everything is quiet and serene. The street lights flicker over the snowy trees; it's so beautiful. In front of the neighbor's house, there's a little snowman, and it looks so funny with its carrot nose and striped scarf. There's not enough snow on the ground, maybe an inch. Whoever built this snowman had to work very hard to shovel enough snow. It makes me laugh. All that hard work, and for what? It'll probably melt by morning. On the other hand, I can identify with the joy of creating something new. This little crooked snowman is a piece of art. It's a piece of life.

We sit in the car for a long time. I'm getting used to feeling Sarah's tongue in my mouth. It's soft and squishy, and I like the way it teases mine, reaching and receding then reaching back. I can't get enough of her.

Her hands unbutton my shirt, and she cups my breasts, her lips nibbling my collarbone.

"Sarah, come in. Spend the night with me." My voice is coarse. I like the way I sound. So sexy.

"Are you sure?"

I don't need to think twice. I've never been as certain of anything as I am right now. I frame her face with my hands. "Well, I've been thinking about it. Sexuality is not straight or gay. It's a spectrum. I don't care about your gender; I care about you as a person."

She stares deep into my soul. "You're incredible, Rachel Davis," she says so close to my lips, it's like I can feel the words echoing in her breath.

The street is so quiet that each little sound is intensified. The soft slam of the trunk when we take out our overnight bags. The way the snow creaks beneath our heels. I try to shush her.

"My mom is probably sleeping," I whisper as I tuck my keys into the lock.

"I won't make a sound," she whispers back. She stands behind me, her hands around my waist.

The house is dark, and I flick the light switch by the door. The sudden brightness makes me squint and sober up from the intoxicating bliss I've been in for the last few hours.

Then I see it. Leftovers of a romantic dinner for two on the dining table; Mom's lacy corset lying on the floor in the hall. I freeze by the door, realizing Mom's probably not alone.

There's a commotion from the master bedroom and Mom's head emerges, a duvet covering her shoulders. I'm guessing she's naked underneath.

"Rachel! You startled me." She sounds terrified and angry.

"Yeah, Mom. Sorry. Things didn't work out…uh…with Dad." It takes me awhile to remember my lie. Sarah giggles behind me, and I'm sure Mom hears her.

"Don't treat me like an idiot," Mom says.

She turns her head, and I hear a muffled sound from inside her bedroom. Then she goes back in, and the door slams behind her.

I hear whispers as Sarah and I tiptoe past it.

"Your mom knows how to party," Sarah whispers when we're safely in my room.

"It's all kind of new to me. She's pretty secretive about

him. I didn't even know he existed until earlier today," I whisper. "Maybe I'll see him in the morning."

"Well, one can only hope," Sarah says, then she takes off her coat, and I forget everything else.

ecca

AT FIRST, I think it's a burglar at the door. But then I sense its Rachel. I don't hear her nor smell her but I know it's her, and I cover myself with the duvet and stick my head out of the door. *What was I going to do if it really was a burglar? Kill him softly with goose down?*

Seeing that it really is Rachel makes me panic. I forget that I've come out in front of my colleagues, in front of Jason. I retreat back to my old behavior.

Lia recovers quickly, relaxing as soon as she hears its Rachel. "So where were we?" she asks. She's lying on my bed completely naked, except for a tie and the strap-on.

Where did she find that tie? I close the door behind me. "Are you crazy? Rachel's here!" I whisper.

"So? She's an adult, right?"

"Shhh." I throw a pillow at her. "She might hear you."

"So?" she repeats.

I'm on the verge of a nervous breakdown. I can't deal with her right now. I just can't.

I pace across the room while talking to myself. *What is she doing here? She's not alone. Is that the funny-looking dude from before? Is it Chase? Are they back together?* My instincts tell me to get rid of Lia before Rachel sees her, but then I'll lose her forever.

"Bex," Lia whispers. I ignore her. "Becca. Stop." She gets off the bed and stops me mid-pace.

"I'm going to leave now," she says. "So you two can talk." She's taking off the harness.

"Don't go," I say and grab her arm. I want her to leave, but I also want her to stay.

"Bexy, I can see how troubled you are. We'll pick this up some other time. No rush." She caresses my arm.

"No. Na-ah." I pass her and continue pacing the room.

"I feel your pain. I don't want to be a burden."

I appreciate her tone; she's on my side. Then a muffled sound comes through the walls. Lia and I look at each other as we both realize that it's the sound of sex.

Lia grins at me. "Well, at least *somebody's* getting some."

"It's not funny! Who's in there with her? Is it Chase? I hope she didn't bring over some random guy." I'm furious.

"Calm down, baby." Lia puts her arms around me. "Don't ruin it for her. She's nineteen, remember? It's time she got into some random guy's pants. Now, come here baby, sit down. You wouldn't have wanted your mama bursting in on you when you had sex in your room, right?" She kisses me on the cheek, and that little kiss awakens my desire.

I must have her. I must have her *now*. I throw her on her back and kiss my way down to her core. She puts her legs on my shoulders and lets me probe her with my tongue.

"Yeah, baby, yeah," she moans. Usually, I go slowly, devour her. But I can't stop. My core pulsates as I put it close to hers. She moves underneath me as we're scissoring, her clit is kissing mine, and it's so good.

On some perverse level, I want Rachel to hear me. I want her to know I that have an active sex life. I come with a roar. Lia arches her back, and I lean forward to catch her nipple with my teeth. That pushes her over the top, and she comes with a series of shrieks.

She doesn't waste any time as she gets up and fastens on the harness with the double-dildos. She pushes one side into her core, and then she positions me on all fours and fucks me doggy style. Her hands are all over my back and buttocks, scratching, caressing.

She sets the rhythm. At first, she goes slowly, so slow I

can feel each nerve being stimulated with every stroke. Each time she pushes, a wave of pleasure washes over me. She feels it too—I can tell by our synced groans. Then she moves faster.

I lift my head to look at her. Her head is tilted back, and her eyes are closed. She looks so beautiful riding me. I reach my hand back to touch her toned abs, and she opens her eyes and smiles at me. It's passionate and loving. She slants forward, and I bend my back until I can reach her face. Our lips join, and we are one.

She goes even faster, and my whole body shakes and twists as I reach the top. I come and come as she goes faster and faster, until I can't take it anymore, and I fall on my face. I'm exhausted, and so is she.

She dives down next to me, laughing and kissing my nose. I still need to catch my breath. I'm sweating, and so is she, her forehead covered with glistening beads.

"Great workout, Bexy," she says, and I giggle before I fall into a deep sleep.

CHAPTER 13

achel

I LIGHT the small reading lamp on my night stand. The room is full of shadows, and I become aware of the decor when Sarah looks around my room. There's a white fur bean bag chair I thought to be adorable at the age of sixteen, and which now acts as a storage place for my stuffed animals, mainly cats, that I couldn't get myself to throw away.

The cat theme kind of rules the room. I have pictures of cute little kittens hanging on the walls and throw pillows with funny cat puns embroidered on them like, aMEOWsment and MEOWcisian. Even my slippers have a picture of grumpy cat, his paw pointing to his mouth.

I'm embarrassed, but Sarah doesn't seem to care. She goes straight to my bookcase and scans the titles. She moves her finger down the spines then picks one out. It's Sylvia Plath's *Ariel*.

"I knew we were soulmates the moment I saw you

reading this in the library," she says. We grin at each other. Her eyes are like two emeralds, glowing in the dark.

I can't take my eyes off of her, but my feet are killing me. I sit down on the bed to take off my boots.

She comes over, leans down, and helps me out. Then she kisses my calves while pulling the pant sleeve up, up over the knees. I hold my breath as her hand slides down under the pant and up my thigh and between my legs. I'm ready for her. Oh, so ready.

She pushes me, and I fall on my back, laughing. I don't know what to do with myself. All I know is that I want this. My thighs are burning with desire.

Sarah works on the belt and unzips me. I raise my head to look at her and notice my panties are showing through the open pants. I'm wearing white cotton briefs. For a second I'm embarrassed by my plain choice of underwear. I'm such a little girl.

She feels my hesitation and stops. "Are you sure?" she whispers.

I nod. "Yes," I say. "I'm certain."

Her hands are gentle when she peels off my pants. My heart is pounding like crazy.

She rests her chin on my panties like she's breathing me in, and it's the sexiest thing anyone has ever done to me. I'm going nuts with desire. I press myself into her face.

She laughs that brassy laugh. Oh, I love her so. And I have to tell her.

"You do?" she asks, her eyes burning in the dark.

"I do. With all my heart, Sarah Walters. You're one of a kind."

"Soulmates?" she asks, and I nod.

She takes off my whities. Slowly. I lift my buttocks to help her.

I've never had anyone go down on me before, and I don't

know what to expect. All I know is that I want her to touch me. To take me.

Her tongue hovers over my clit. Then it's like a thousand bolts of lightning shoot through my body all at once. I forget my mother is in the next room when I moan heavily. I didn't know I was even capable of producing these wild noises. I spread my legs as wide as I can. Sarah gets it; she continues to lick my folds. I don't know what she's doing, but everywhere she touches it's like a firecracker's been popped inside my brain. I've never felt like this before.

Suddenly, I'm all shivery. My legs twitch uncontrollably, and I scream with pleasure. She licks me quicker and harder until I can't take it anymore and put my hands in her hair.

She waits for me to float back. When I open my eyes, her smiling face is next to mine. Her lips glisten with my juices.

"That was…" I can't find a way to describe my experience. "Amazing," I finally say.

She laughs that laugh I love so much. And I tell her that as I caress her cheek. Then I slide down; I want to return the favor. But she stops me.

"I just want to cuddle, okay?"

I'm puzzled. "I want to make you come."

"I know. But I'm hard to please," Sarah says. "I'll teach you everything in time. Don't worry about it." She kisses my nose, and I can smell myself on her breath. It drives me crazy, and I'm all horny and ready for her again.

"You forget one thing," I say as I straddle her. My voice sounds husky, and I like it. I *love* it. "I've read your poems. I know exactly what you like."

I crush my lips on hers and push my tongue deep into her mouth. She moans as I squash my body against hers. I wander my hands over her body, squeezing her breasts as I nibble her neck. I find my way into her panties, and she's wet with anticipation. She grabs my hands and guides me as I explore her folds. I stroke her clit with my index finger and she tilts her head back. She looks so beautiful. I lean over and kiss her collarbone.

"Fuck me," she says, her voice gruff and so sexy. I slide one finger into her, then another one. She starts moving against my fingers. Her hands scratch my back, and she pulls my hair as I finger her hard and fast. I can see she's ready to reach her climax, and I'm going to come with her. I stroke her clit with my thumb, and she clenches my hands with her thighs as the orgasm shakes her body. It's amazing. For me, too.

She hugs me and buries her face in my shoulder. I hear her sob and feel tears.

"What's wrong?" I ask.

She shakes her head. "It's just...you're so good with my body," she says. "You *know* me."

I smile. "I do." I'm so happy when we cuddle close, and as we drift into sleep, I believe this is the best day I've ever had.

CHAPTER 14

ecca

IT'S ALREADY light outside when I wake up. Lia is lying on her stomach next to me, her unkempt hair covering her face. Her breath is light, and I can tell she's still fast asleep. It's only 6:30 a.m., quite early for a Saturday, but I hear noises in the kitchen. *Rachel.* She's trying to sneak out her boyfriend, and the fury from last night rebuilds inside me. I need to teach her a lesson, tell her what's what. I also want to take a good look at the boy she brought home last night. *Is it Chase?* I hope it's Chase.

achel

I WAKE UP ABRUPTLY. It takes a minute for me to remember what's going on. With my eyes still closed, I reach my hand to the other side of the bed. It's empty. Now I have to open my eyes. The glare of my alarm clock is right in front me. 6:03 a.m. on a Saturday morning.

Just great. *Did I dream everything that happened last night?* It seemed so real. I turn to my other side, and there's Sarah, sitting on the furry bean bag chair. She's writing quickly, the pen flying over the notebook she's holding. Her phone is tucked in her slouchy, its flashlight on. With her head down, only the notebook is illuminated. I observe her for a while. She's so absorbed, she doesn't notice my stare. It's beautiful to watch her work.

When she finally lifts her eyes from the page, the flash-light blinds me. I raise my hand to cover my eyes.

"Oh, sorry." She turns if off. "Did I wake you?" She crawls back into bed and curls up next to me. Her body radiates heat, and it feels good to cuddle.

"I was up all night," she says happily. She seems inspired; her eyes are glistening.

"The curse is off," she grins. "I wrote an epic poem. I think it's my best work yet. And it's because of you." She kisses me softly then closes her eyes. She looks so serene.

I can't get back to sleep; I'm curious about her poem. Is it about me? Is it another verse of her long sexual epic? Slowly, I pull away from her. I don't want her to wake up and catch me peeking. Her notebook is filled with doodles and random words, some of them circled. This is her process. It's so very raw. I feel bad for invading her privacy. I put the notebook down exactly as I found it. Now I'm too ashamed to crawl back into bed with her.

ecca

RACHEL'S WEARING her kitten pajamas. She looks so innocent, which is quite a contrast to the noises she made last night. She's cleared the dining table of last night's leftovers, and now she's sitting with a steamy mug in front of her. It looks like she's been waiting for me.

"Morning," I say.

She looks up from her mug. Her face is glowing, and I'm overwhelmed. I don't recall when I last saw her this happy. The speech I've prepared fades away, along with my anger. I'm filled with tender bliss. After all, this is what I've always wanted—for her to be happy.

"Mother." She nods, acknowledging my presence.

"Daughter," I say in return and grab a chair opposite her.

She chuckles. "Coffee? I just made a fresh brew."

Well, this is a first. I thought she didn't know how to operate the coffee maker.

She gets up and pours me a cup.

It's good. "Who are you, and what have you done with my daughter?"

She smiles. There's a mischievous sparkle in her eyes, a playful hint in her grin.

"Is there something you want to tell me?" I squint at her.

"Is there something *you* want to tell *me*?" she shoots right back.

"I heard you. Last night."

She nods. "Yep. Heard you too."

I don't know what to do. I circle the rim of my cup with my finger. She takes a sip from her cup and sighs. It's a satisfied sigh. She used to sigh like that when she was a baby and ate something yummy. She's not that kid anymore.

We sit quietly for a few minutes. A ray of sunshine penetrates the kitchen window and blinds us. It seems like the storm has cleared out.

"So?" I break the silence. "Are you going to tell me where you were last night, you rascal?"

She smiles. With the sunlight in her hair, she looks golden, and I'm swept with motherly love. "Believe it or not, I was in a community center in Joliet."

"Community center in Joliet? Really? What did you do down there? Rob the place?"

Her shoulders drop. "Sorry I freaked you out last night. I should have called, let you know I was coming."

"Tell me what you were up to, and I might forgive you."

She smiles that mischievous smile again. "I promise to tell you everything after you introduce me to your fella."

"My fella?"

"Come on, Mom. I'm not stupid. I know it's been going on for months now. Why didn't you tell me about him?"

"Him?" I repeat after her. I'm not sure what to say, although my gut tells me this is the perfect time to tell her.

With the playful sunshine in her hair and her easygoing attitude, she's ripe and ready and asking about it. But I'm terribly frightened. What will I do if she doesn't accept my relationship with Lia?

The memory of her expression when she stood right here in the kitchen and told me straight to my face she didn't like Lia as a trainer horrifies me. She didn't like her as a trainer, so will she accept her as my partner? After she finds out, there's no going back. I want to prolong this moment of happiness before everything shatters.

Before I'm forced to make hard decisions. Before I'm forced to choose between my daughter and the love of my life.

achel

I'm SLIGHTLY OFFENDED. Why doesn't she want to tell me about her new relationship? Right as I'm about to raise my voice and express my displeasure, someone emerges from the hall.

Mom is all jumpy and flushed. "Rachel, "Mom says, "You remember Lia?"

I don't understand. "Can't say that I do."

"Lia. From the gym. Our personal trainer," she says as if that should mean something.

"Lia. From the gym." I mutter as I try to recall that one class I took six months ago. "But why is she here? Are you having an early morning workout?"

Mom looks confused. I stare at Mom and Lia as they glance at each other. Lia's wearing boxers and a T-shirt. She looks like she just got out of bed.

And then everything clicks. Lia. From the gym. *She's* Mom's new fella. I start laughing. It's so funny. I mean, what are the odds?

Mom looks miserable; my reaction clearly hurt her. I try to calm myself down and explain. I'm sure that once I tell her about Sarah, she'll get why it's so funny. I point at Lia and say, "She's—" and then another burst of laughter stops me from talking.

Lia puts her hand on Mom's shoulder, and Mom holds her hand. They look so cool, like they belong together. And I'd say that, if I could only catch my breath.

ecca

RACHEL'S REACTION SHOCKS ME. It's not at all what I'd expected. I could have handled contempt, even disgust. But the way she laughs, it's humiliating. It's shameful. It's a disgrace. Having Lia by my side reassures me that we're fine; we'll survive this.

But I get angrier as Rachel keeps on laughing. I'm about to get up and smack her face. God knows it's not the first time I've felt like doing that, but it will be the first time I've acted on it.

Fortunately, Lia's holding my hand and patting my shoulder; she can feel the rage in my tensed shoulders. When I meet her eyes, she nods. She got why I was afraid to tell Rachel, but that doesn't stop me from being ashamed and embarrassed at my daughter's behavior. And at the same time, this stupid response makes my connection with Lia stronger. We are united.

Then someone new approaches the table. Lia's hand falls off my shoulder, and she starts laughing too.

At first, I don't get it, but then I see Rachel's lover, and I join the laughter. Pretty soon the four of us are grabbing our stomachs. We laugh so hard, it hurts. Rachel is crying with laughter, and the other woman is holding her stomach too.

When we finally settle down, Rachel makes introductions. Her girlfriend, Sarah, shakes my hand. "You have a great daughter, Mrs. Davis. She's one of the most promising poets I've ever met."

I give Rachel a quick glance. *A poet?*

She flushes and makes a gesture saying, *I'll tell you about it later.*

"Call me Becca," I say. "I haven't been Mrs. Davis for a while now."

Rachel

MOM LOOKS SURPRISED when Sarah enters. She looks at me and then looks back at Sarah. By this time, Lia has caught on to my wild laughter and the both of us are cackling hysterically. It's so ridiculous, really. Yet, so great.

"Mom, Lia, this is Sarah," I say when I can finally catch my breath. I flush. I don't know if I should introduce her as my girlfriend or my mentor. We haven't discussed that.

Sarah looks at me.

"Lia?" she mouths silently, her eyes wide. She's as surprised as I am. But she recovers quickly. Actually, she handles it better than I do.

Sarah smiles at Mom and Lia, extending her hand for a shake. I guess I should have done that too—shake Lia's hand instead of laughing hysterically. And I intend to do so when Sarah suddenly mentions my poems. Mom gives me a weird look, and I feel so awkward, like a child who's gotten caught cheating on a test. So I just sit there and pull my sleeves down. Out of the blue, without any real reason, Lia screams. It's a short scream of surprise. She says, "Excuse me for a second," before disappearing into the master bedroom.

Mom puts her hand on my shoulder. "A poet?" she asks, smiling. She looks proud. It's an unexpectedly pleasant surprise.

I shrug like I want to say, *it's not a big deal*. Sarah slides into a chair next to me. She looks sleepy. "You people always wake up this early on a Saturday?" she mumbles and rests her head on her hands. The sun plays with her hair, and I move my hand to caress her neck.

Mom's still staring at me, smiling. "Will you let me read your poems?"

I nod. It's not at all what I expected. I'd thought she'd be all judgmental and rebuke me for choosing that path. Instead, her support fills me with delicate warmth and love.

"Why didn't you tell me about Lia?" I whisper.

"Because you hated her after that class we had. You said she reminded you of a serial killer."

I don't recall that. I'm surprised she put so much weight on a random remark I made so long ago. I'm about to say something when Lia reappears.

She's wearing a pantsuit, and what looks like one of Dad's old ties. Her hair is gathered into a tight ponytail. She doesn't take her eyes off Mom as she marches forward. She looks so much in love.

"I know it's probably too soon, but…" She says and kneels down in front of Mom and takes a ring out of her pocket. She doesn't say anything. Her eyes are full of tears.

Mom puts her hands over her mouth. She nods repeatedly. "Yes. Yes." She sobs and leans over to kiss her bride.

I rush over to hug them. First Lia, then Mom. Then it's a group hug with the three of us. I'm so happy, I can't find the words to express my joy.

Then Sarah wakes up and slowly lifts her head from the table. She looks at the three of us with wonder.

"What did I miss?" she asks with a heavy tone.

It's so funny, but I'm all out of laughs.

"Rachel's going to have a new mom," Lia says. She makes me feel so welcome.

"Well, congratulations!" Sarah says. She's still sleepy, but her eyes are sparkling, and my heart overflows with love.

It's weird to kiss her in front of Mom, and it's even weirder to see Mom kissing her fiancé. But I'll have to get used to it, and I know that I will.

Hey, maybe I'll even write a poem about it.

- The End -

Want more of Becca and Lia?
Scan this QR code to get the FREE prequel:

falling for Lia!

If you liked this book please consider **leaving a review** as an act of kindness for other readers like you. Thank you!

ABOUT BETH LOURE

Beth Loure is a 19th century soul living inside a millennial body. She longs for the simpler times and is still looking for a Mrs. Darcy. Beth Lives by the coast with a companion gray parrot named Johnny, who keeps reminding her to sit down and write. With these exact words. When she's not writing or reading you can find her attending the roses in her garden.

You can find her here:
bethloure.com
info@bethloure.com

The Flower Triangle

Coming Soon: Russian Bride

Rose **is** the first book of the **Flower Triangle** trilogy. Turn a page to read the first chapter.

ROSE: FIRST CHAPTER

*R*ose's eyes were still closed, but her other senses were waking up. A fire crackled nearby; she could feel its warmth. That was nice, unlike the stench of mildew that made her nose twitch. Alarm bells started ringing inside her head. *Wake up. Wake up.*

Rose inhaled deeply. There were other smells in the air. Good ones. She relaxed a bit as she tried to distinguish them from one another. There was the unmistakable nutty aroma of roasted chestnuts and the mild smell of fresh oysters. Rose sniffed the air. She could sense a hint of chocolate, and by the tickle in her nostrils, she knew that a fine bottle of Cabernet had been recently uncorked close by. Her stomach rumbled. *I'm so hungry*, she thought and smiled at the promise of a good meal with all her favorite foods.

She tried to move, to shift her position in her tight blanket-cocoon. It was a habit adopted in early childhood — to cuddle inside her comforter like one would in a sleeping bag. She would make the cocoon so snug she couldn't move her hands or feet, but this felt tighter.

Where's Reed? Rose thought, still half asleep. He doesn't

like it when I steal the entire comforter for myself. The logical part of her brain, which was already awake, tried to make sense of the situation in the form of a story. *Reed. Oh, sweet, sweet Reed. He let me sleep in while he's making my favorite food for dinner.*

A slow grin spread upon Rose's face.

Then she remembered. Reed. Dahlia. The mental image of the two came back to torment her.

She opened her eyes. The smile turned into a scared frown. The warm feeling turned into a frigid fright. She shivered. Goosebumps crawled up her spine.

This can't be true. I'm not really here. I must still be asleep, and this is a terrible nightmare.

"Wake up, wake up," Rose murmured to herself.

She closed her eyes and reopened them, only to find out that nothing had changed.

She was still standing in what seemed to be a large cave. The walls and the high ceiling had a rough, rocky surface, and the floor beneath Rose's bare feet had a sandy feel. Moving was impossible; she was restrained. Her legs were spread apart and chained at the ankles to what looked like the lower part of a wooden X. The intersection pressed against the small of her back, then opened again. She could feel the hardness of the wood behind her shoulder blades.

Rose's wrists were pinned to her thighs with soft, fuzzy ropes. And she was naked. Completely. The only thing she was wearing was the golden necklace with the cross medallion she got from Uncle Henry for her confirmation. It hung low between her breasts like it always did. It was the one thing she never took off.

Pure panic crawled through Rose's veins. She stood still for a moment and then began rattling the shackles vigorously. She stretched her hands in a helpless effort to loosen the ropes. For nothing. There was no give.

"Help," she whispered, and then the whisper became a bellow. "Help me," she yelled. Her voice echoed back from the rocky walls. Her call remained unanswered.

She heard another woman voice screaming, "Let me go! Please, let me go home. I'll do anything. Just let me go!"

I'm not alone here, Rose thought, and that thought was paralyzing. *I'm going to die in here. I'm going to die, and no one will ever know.*

A few weeks ago, Rose had made an attempt to end her own life. She was ready to face death and was spared.

It can't be, Rose thought, *I couldn't have been saved only to die here.*

The other voice turned into quiet sobs. Rose asked, "Hello? Who's there?"

Nobody answered. There was more screaming.

Rose shivered, thinking about the pain the other woman was suffering. Was she due for a similar fate? Would she be the one screaming like that?

"Oh, yes. Yes. YES. YESSSSS," the other woman cried, and then she screamed again. Rose wasn't so sure she was being tortured.

"Hmmm…Hello?" Rose dared ask when the screaming stopped. "I'm being held here too. Hello?"

No answer. Not even an acknowledgment of being heard.

Rose breathed deeply. *Stay calm*, she said to herself, *stay calm*. She began examining her surroundings.

The cave was poorly lit, with torches standing around the walls. She twisted her neck as much as she could and noticed a hearth behind her back. A few heavy logs were crackling in the fire. It looked very similar to the hearth Reed had built in their house. Suddenly, Rose felt like a huge stone had been put on her chest, as big as the boulder to her left that blocked her vision of that part of the cave. The weight was so heavy she couldn't breathe.

She recognized the feeling. It was the yearning for Reed. The thought of never seeing him again was unbearable. Although she was being held captive, although she might be facing an agonizing death, she thought only of not being able to see Reed again, to hold him in her arms, feel his skin against hers, and smell his distinguished aroma of Paco Rabanne fragrance mixed with sweat. She hated him for what he had done to her, but she never stopped loving him. The thought of dying without telling him that was intolerable. Hot tears filled her eyes.

On the far right end of the cave, there was an opening in the wall. To Rose's foggy eyes, it looked like a black hole. She couldn't see beyond it.

A massive table was set near the opening, upon which a nice spread of wines, spirits, meats, and fruits was organized tastefully. There were some steamy pots on hot plates, and in the middle, a huge chocolate fountain dripped brown nectar and made a wonderful dripping sound as the melted chocolate fell into the pool below. Rose's stomach rumbled again.

I'm so hungry. How long have I been here? And how did I get here?

"Hello?" she called again. "Someone there?"

Her voice echoed from the walls. The screaming woman's voice from before screamed again, yelling, "Oh my God, we're all going to die!" in a high-pitched voice.

A shiver crossed Rose's body. She closed her eyes and murmured a prayer.

"Lord, have mercy on us. Christ, hear us. Christ, graciously hear us." Rose murmured with her eyes closed. At home, she used to hold her communion cross on her lips when she prayed. It gave her comfort. It got warm when she prayed, indicating that her prayers had been accepted. Praying now wasn't the same without it. It was like walking in the dark with no torch to lead her way.

"Purest Mother Mary, let your name be ever on my lips. Delay not, blessed Lady, to rescue me whenever I call on you."

Rose kept humming her prayers devotionally.

Then, her prayers were answered. A sweet, angelic voice whispered in her ears, "You must forgive to be redeemed."

The voice was so soft and light that Rose didn't know if she'd really heard it, or if she was hallucinating.

"Salvation comes with condonation," the velvety voice spoke again.

Another set of hot tears filled Rose's eyes. She knew exactly what she was meant to do.

"I forgive!" she yelled with all the air she had in her lungs.

Rose closed her eyes. The image of Reed and Dahlia doing that terrible act on her wedding bed kept tormenting her. "I forgive you, Reed. I forgive you, Dahlia." She knew it wasn't a genuine pardon. She was still angry and resentful.

Whenever she closed her eyes, she could see Dahlia, kneeling on the edge of the bed, her curvy ass rippling. And Reed standing behind her, pants around his ankles while his cock pounded in and out of Dahlia's anus.

It was blasphemy. It was the picture of pure evil. And it was weirdly arousing.

Rose wanted desperately to erase that mental image, but she couldn't. It was as if the image was imprinted on her retinas by a blinding sun. She could always see it, whenever she closed her eyes, or when she turned her head quickly. Dahlia and Reed were there, in her blurry vision. They were laughing a demonic laugh. Rose knew they hadn't been laughing when she caught them fornicating. It was her mind playing tricks, putting devil horns on Reed's forehead. Putting bleeding vampire teeth on Dahlia. Putting that dampness between her legs.

Rose wept heavily. She wouldn't be able to fully forgive as the angel had told her.

"Oh Lord, please guide me to the way of forgiveness," she prayed.

The angelic voice spoke again. This time it said, "Prepare yourself. The sex therapist is coming. He will cure you."

The sex therapist! Of course! Rose was so relieved. She burst into noisy sobs of relief.

Click here to get *Rose* for free.